THE DISGRACED BRIDE

THE SPINSTERS GUILD (BOOK 2)

ROSE PEARSON

LANDON HILL MEDIA

THE DISGRACED BRIDE: A REGENCY ROMANCE

The Spinsters Guild

(Book 2)

By

Rose Pearson

THE DISGRACED BRIDE

"*I* hardly think that this is the right time to go about such an endeavor."

Miss Emma Bavidge looked down at her hands, her heart twisting in her chest.

"I must have her married off," she heard her father, Viscount Hawkridge, state. "She must be able to have some sort of future."

"And just who would look at her?" came the sharp, shrill voice of her spinster aunt, Lady Mitchell. "There is very little chance that even a single gentleman will so much as glance at her. No, you are asking me too much, brother."

A long silence followed. Emma twisted her fingers together, breathing slowly and carefully as she fought to keep her composure. She knew full well that to go to society now would be rather difficult after what had occurred only last year, but if she did not go now, then her chances of remaining a spinster increased dramatically. She did not have the beauty of face that captured every gentleman's attention and had her declared a 'diamond of the first water.' Nor did she have a large dowry with which to entice a gentleman, for her father had made certain of that. There was, as her aunt had suggested, very little chance that Emma would be able to find a suitor, but surely, she had to be given the opportunity to try? It had to be better than remaining at home, whiling away the days of summer and feeling as though her life were slipping away from her, fearing that she would be as she was now for the rest of her days.

Closing her eyes, Emma let out her breath slowly, her hands suddenly tightening into fists as a spike of anger slammed painfully into her heart. None of this was her doing. This was all entirely her father's mistake, and now she had to bear the consequences of it. It felt most unfair, for why should the shame of her father's behavior cling to her? *She* had done nothing wrong, for she had always made certain to keep herself within the realms of propriety, but regardless of that, it seemed that she too was to be washed with the dirt that now clung to her father.

"I should have found a way to keep her in London last season."

Her father's voice was low and muffled, and Emma had to strain to hear, knowing that she ought not to be eavesdropping outside her father's study but finding it impossible to step away. She had to know what was being said.

"You did what you could," replied Lady Mitchell in a tired fashion. "You had responsibilities here."

"No," Lord Hawkridge replied angrily, a sudden thump making Emma's heart jump in her chest. Had her father slammed a hand onto the desk in frustration?

"No," Lord Hawkridge said again. "I have been selfish. I did not take Emma to town when she was first of age. Instead, I told myself that I could not afford it, what with the state of my home and estate. That was naught more than a lie, sister." His voice dropped low, clearly upset. "I wanted to keep as much of my wealth for my own purposes; that is the truth of it. I did not want to spend money on my daughter, for I knew she would need new gowns and the like in order to make her debut in London. And then, last year, when I took her with me to make her debut, I chose instead to bring such shame upon the family name that I had no other recourse but to remove both myself and her from London before only a fortnight had passed. What a cruel, selfish father I have been!"

Emma pressed one hand to her mouth, tears pooling in the corners of her eyes. Her father had never once admitted to any such thing to her, and she was quite certain that, had she been in the room, he would not have said anything of the sort. However, to hear it from him, to know that he was aware of his wrongdoing and just how it now affected him, brought her heart a good deal of sorrow. It was too late for apologies. Time had marched past them both, leaving her older and all the more afraid that she would become a spinster, forced to remain with her father until his last days and then to seek out charity from amongst her relatives. What had been done by Lord

Hawkridge had left a heavy load upon her back, and words of regret did not take any of her burden away.

"Will you stop feeling sorry for yourself?"

The brash words of her aunt pulled Emma from her sorrow, making her blink rapidly until all her tears had disappeared.

"You have behaved foolishly and left the burden of responsibility upon your daughter," Emma's aunt continued. "And now you seek out my help to try to ensure that your daughter finds a suitor after all—which is an unenviable task, I assure you!" She tutted, clearly still displeased with being asked to do so. "Quite how I am meant to hold my head up in society when you are known to be my brother is going to be quite another matter, however."

"Then you will come to our aid?" Lord Hawkridge asked, sounding hopeful. "You will do as I have asked of you?"

Emma held her breath, waiting for her aunt's response. She bit her lip, closing her eyes tightly as the seconds dragged out before her. Her aunt was obviously still considering what would be best to do—not best for Emma but rather for herself. It would be difficult for Lady Mitchell to appear in London society also, for people would whisper about her and her association with Lord Hawkridge.

"Oh, very well," Lady Mitchell sighed, sounding exasperated. "I shall take Emma to town with me and ensure she is chaperoned and the like."

The sound of a scraping chair told Emma that her father had gotten to his feet, perhaps grasping her aunt's hands to thank her.

"You are truly one of the kindest ladies I know," Lord Hawkridge said, his voice filled with relief. "Thank you, dear sister. I know that Emma will appreciate your willingness even more than I."

Emma did not hear her aunt's response. She was battling tears, tears of relief that threatened to run down her cheeks and sobs that stuck in her throat. Turning away from the door of her father's study, she moved quickly, but as quietly as she could, hurrying away to her rooms where she might find solitude.

She was to go to London after all. She was to have the chance to find a suitor, to make a match that would bring her happiness and a future worthy of a gentleman's daughter. Yes, it would be difficult, and yes, she would have to deal with many people questioning whether or not she ought to even be stepping into society again, but Emma was determined to make the most of her time in London. She would hold her head high, she told herself, pushing open the door of her bedchamber. She would ignore the whispers, ignore the dark looks and the rumors that would swirl about her, safe in the knowledge that she had done nothing wrong. Surely, somewhere, there had to be even one gentleman who would not count her father's sins against her? One gentleman who would look at her with an unhindered gaze, who would consider her for who she was and not what her father had done. Sitting down on the edge of her bed, Emma closed her eyes and pressed her hands together as though in prayer.

"Let me be able to find such a gentleman," she whispered aloud, her eyes brimming with tears all over again. "I do not ask for love nor affection, but only for a kindness of heart and a joy of spirit that will be contented with someone such as me."

Surely, that was not too much to ask.

CHAPTER ONE

"I fear my aunt has quite given up on me."

Miss Sarah Crosby linked arms with Emma and sighed heavily. "I am sorry for that, Emma."

Emma tried to shrug off such a thing with an easy smile and a lift of her shoulders, but neither came without difficulty. The truth was, the way that her aunt had treated her this last fortnight had made things all the more difficult for Emma, instead of aiding her in what was already a hard situation.

"She wished to remove herself from the..." Miss Crosby frowned, trying to find the words. "The rumors that seem to cling to you," she finished, still frowning. "Is that not so?"

Knowing that it was simply the way of Miss Crosby to be blunt in her speech and manner, Emma gave her a slightly rueful nod. "My aunt agreed to help me, agreed to ensure that I managed to traverse society without too much difficulty, but I believe the idea seemed easier than actually being amongst the *beau monde* and seeing how they treat me." She shook her head, a lump beginning to form in her throat. "When I arrived back in London, whispers began from the very moment I set foot within society." Swallowing hard, she tried to smile, but the corner of her lips did not even quirk. "The *ton* is a cruel creature, Sarah."

Her friend sighed heavily and nodded. "Indeed it is," she agreed, softly. "I am sorry to hear that you have had such trouble."

"I have, at least, received invitations to various events," Emma replied, trying to find hope and encouragement in even the smallest of things. "However, sometimes I fear that such invitations are given in the knowledge that my presence will only add to the chatter surrounding someone's soiree or ball." Sighing, she adjusted her bonnet carefully, even though it already sat perfectly, wanting to cover up her struggle to contain her emotions. "And the same can be said for the gentlemen that seek to dance with me." Closing her eyes for a moment, Emma took in a gulp of air, steadying her composure. "I was foolish enough to believe that such gentlemen found me engaging enough to seek me out at a ball or the like. Instead, I have come to learn that they want nothing more than the notoriety that comes with dancing with someone such as myself, whose reputation is darkened due to the behavior of my father last season." The unfairness of it all bit at her hard, but with an effort, Emma pushed such feelings aside. There was no use in lingering on them, for it would do her no good whatsoever.

"There is not even one gentleman who has shown

you any genuine interest?" Miss Crosby asked, looking across at Emma as they walked together. "None?"

Emma hesitated before she shook her head. There was one gentleman she had caught watching her on more than one occasion these last two weeks, but he had never approached her, had never sought her out to dance. The way his eyes had lingered on hers as she had looked steadily back at him still took her by surprise whenever she thought of it, for even though he had not introduced himself, there was something about his gaze that would not leave her. Oft times she caught herself thinking of him, not certain what it was about his manner that intrigued her so. Most likely, he was nothing more than any other gentleman had been—interested in her for the sole reason of adding to the whispers and rumors that swirled around her.

Miss Crosby sighed again, bringing Emma out of her confused thoughts. "The *ton* are not kind," she muttered, reminding Emma that she was not the only one with difficulties when it came to society as a whole. "What can be done about it?"

Emma bit her lip, not quite certain what she could do. To say she could do nothing would be to make herself quite helpless, to make herself entirely at the *ton*'s mercy, and she did not want to allow that. But what could she do? She could continue as she was, praying that someone would consider her despite the fact that her reputation was so blackened, or she could attempt to seek out more help from somewhere else. Her aunt clearly was rather displeased that she had agreed to help Emma back into society, perhaps having not expected to find so much difficulty when it came to her niece, and so often kept well away from Emma even when they attended the same event together. She was distancing herself, clearly trying to play the part of a concerned yet unhappy aunt who was doing what she could for her unfortunate niece whilst remaining aloof and cold towards her. It was a strange role to play, but her aunt was doing it very well indeed, which left Emma alone to try to navigate through the icy waters of London high society.

"If only there were someone who had managed to do what I now consider to be almost impossible," Miss Crosby murmured, speaking aloud but as though she spoke to herself. "If only we had an acquaintance to whom we might turn to for advice and aid."

Emma's brow furrowed, her mind suddenly filled with what Miss Crosby had said. "We have no such acquaintance," she said, slowly, "but what if we could make one?"

Miss Crosby looked at her in surprise, their steps slow as they meandered through the park. "What do you mean, Emma?"

Biting her lip, Emma hesitated and then sat down on a bench, gesturing for her friend to do the same. "Have you heard of Lady Smithton?"

Miss Crosby's eyes flared in surprise. "Lady Smithton? Yes, I believe so. She has only just returned to town after some time away."

"Time in mourning, yes," Emma said, slowly, recalling the first time she had heard about Lady Smithton, although, as yet, she had not been introduced to the lady and did not even know what she looked like. "Her husband died, and she has returned to London, even though there have been whispers that she was involved in his death in some such way."

A line formed between Miss Crosby's brows as she frowned. "I have heard the rumors, of course, but gave them no attention," she replied, carefully. "Lady Smithton seems to navigate through the *ton* without any difficulties whatsoever. She brushes aside the gossip and holds her head high."

"You have seen her?" Emma asked, eagerly. "What does she do that gains the *ton*'s respect, even though she has so many gossip mongers eager to tear her to pieces?"

Miss Crosby considered this for a moment, then shrugged. "I cannot say precisely, for I have only watched her from afar. It is as though she does not care what *ton* might say about her; she gives it not even a moment of consideration. In proving this in her demeanor, she seems to float above such things in some way." She waved a hand, evidently frustrated. "I am not explaining it very well, I know, but she seems untroubled by the rumors, and therefore, there are those who greatly admire her."

This was precisely what Emma wanted to hear. "Then mayhap she would be inclined to help us, should we ask her."

Miss Crosby's frown drew down still further. "But we are not acquainted with her," she said, stating the obvious difficulty with Emma's suggestion. "Nor do we know anyone able to introduce her to us."

"Then we speak to her without introduction," Emma replied firmly, seeing that this was the only way forward. "It is not the correct way, I grant you, but if we do nothing, then all that will remain is a difficult few months of the continuing season and a creeping despondency that we will be left without any hope whatsoever." She lifted one brow and held her friend's gaze. "I do not wish for that to occur, Sarah."

Miss Crosby considered this for some moments, her eyes searching Emma's face as she thought.

"I will struggle to do most anything, given that I must be with my cousin most of the time," she said slowly, her brows still knotted. "I am not certain that Lady Smithton will be able to help me in any way, even if I was to ask her."

Emma, feeling a slow-growing sense of hope, smiled at her friend. "Then why not allow me to speak to Lady Smithton first?" she suggested, seeing how Miss Crosby's frown began to fade. "I shall introduce myself and see if Lady Smithton is in any way amiable to the idea of helping us traverse society. If she is not, then there is no harm done to either of us. Your cousin will have no reason to think ill of you, for you have not been the one to introduce yourself to a lady of Lady Smithton's standing without an acquaintance present to do so, and I am certain that my aunt will not care!"

Miss Crosby gave her a wry smile, nodding slowly. "And if she is agreeable?"

"Then I shall tell you at once, and you shall make your own introductions," Emma suggested, feeling more and more satisfied with this plan. "What say you, Sarah? I shall not go ahead if you do not think it wise."

Miss Crosby did not hesitate, however, but began to nod fervently. "I think it is an excellent idea," she said, making Emma smile. "I must hope that Lady Smithton will be agreeable to such a thing, however." Her look of hope began to fade. "What if she does not wish to help us?"

"Then we cannot say we have not tried," Emma replied, firmly. "I must hope that Lady Smithton has a kind heart, for she must surely understand just how difficult it is to make one's way through society when there are rumors and whispers abounding!" Lady Smithton was able to throw aside such gossip without seemingly any difficulty, and it was this that made Emma hope the lady would be willing to, at the very least, give them some advice. "I do not know when I shall see her next nor when I will be able to approach her to explain what it is I am hoping for, but I have every intention of doing so just as soon as I am able." She gave Miss Crosby a broad smile, seeing the light flickering in her friend's eyes and realizing that Miss Crosby felt the same small hope that now lit her own heart.

"Then I will confess to be rather excited at the prospect," Miss Crosby said, getting to her feet and brushing down her skirts. "You will keep me informed, will you not?"

"Of course I will," Emma replied, warmly, also rising. "You must return to your cousin now, I think?"

Miss Crosby grimaced but nodded. She was practically a chaperone to her cousin, who was only a few years younger than Miss Crosby herself but who had such a beauty about her that the *ton* was already speaking of her as a diamond of the first water. "Yes," she muttered, clearly frustrated. "I must return to her. I believe we are to take tea with some gentleman or other and, of course, I must attend with her to ensure that everything is quite proper." She rolled her eyes at Emma, who could not help but laugh.

"Let us hope that Lady Smithton will be able to advise you as to how to extract yourself from such a role," she said, laughing, as she linked arms with her friend again. "Or that your cousin finds a match very quickly so that you are free to pursue such a thing for yourself."

Miss Crosby did not answer but let out a small sigh that Emma understood too well. It was a sigh that spoke of sadness over lost opportunities, over the difficulties that they had both endured in different ways. It was a pain that filled her heart over and over again, each time a gentleman stepped away from her or allowed his gaze to merely brush over her without showing any particular interest. But no, Emma determined, lifting her chin and finding a new resolve filling her heart. She would not allow herself to be torn down by frustration and pain. Instead, she would allow herself to hope; to hope that Lady Smithton would be the answer to their troubles, that she would be their one light in what had been a very dark few weeks.

And it was a hope that bolstered her confidence with every step she took.

CHAPTER TWO

*V*iscount Nathaniel Morton decided, quite firmly, that he did not want to be here this evening. The ball was already well underway, and the crush of guests made even the thought of stepping into the crowd more than a little unwelcome. He could not simply turn on his heel and step away, however, for his friend, Lord White, would be most displeased if he were to do so given that he had only just arrived.

Nathaniel sighed to himself and made to run his hand through his thick, dark hair, only to stop himself from doing so when he recalled just how long it had taken to settle it. It was a bad habit of his, for he often did so when he was frustrated or irritated by something or another, but given that he was in his very finest clothes and needed to ensure that he remained as pristine as possible for as long as possible, thrusting his hand through his hair was not a good idea.

Sighing, he turned around, not wanting to descend the three small steps that would take him into the ballroom but finding that he had little option open to him. Behind him was the door that would lead him back to where had come from, and to either side there seemed to be nothing other than small alcoves, both of which were rather poorly lit. Aware that he would have to soon enter the ballroom regardless of whether he wished to or not, Nathaniel moved hurriedly into one of the alcoves, pressing himself into the shadows as the door opened again to admit a few more guests.

A tall, gray-haired lady walked past him, talking rapidly with another lady who appeared to be of similar age. Two others followed them, both young ladies who were clad in gowns of light cream or white. Nathaniel gave them no more than a cursory glance, thinking to himself that he was a little too old to be interested in debutantes. Yes, he would have to consider matrimony and, therefore, seek out a wife for himself, but a debutante would not do. They were much too flighty, much too easily overcome by almost anything and everything that the *ton* provided. No, he required a lady who was a little more balanced than a debutante. Mayhap someone who was on their second or third season, who knew precisely what a gentleman such as he was seeking in a wife and who would remain levelheaded and entirely proper throughout their courtship and engagement. He did not want a creature who thought only of her gowns, or who lost herself in a flurry of excitement over some new bonnet or other. Nor did he want someone who found their happiness in speaking gossip or rumors about others amongst the *ton*. His stomach twisted at the thought, knowing that there were those amongst society who sought to do nothing more than spread the latest titbits from one person to the next. No, he had no time for that sort of creature.

A sudden sound startled him. So caught up had he been in looking after the debutantes and reflecting upon just how little they interested him that he had not seen that the other alcove now held someone within it. The young lady was pressing herself into the shadows, just as he had done, and her hands were clasped tightly together in front of her. She did not look at him but rather let her gaze stretch out towards the crowd, her lips pressed together. Was she afraid of the *ton* for some reason?

Nathaniel found his interest growing steadily as he continued to watch her, wondering at her audacious behavior, for a young lady ought not to be standing alone in a place such as this! She ought to be with her chaperone or her mother, depending on who she had attended with—but this young lady showed no intention of hurrying after those who had walked in with her. Not quite able to make out her features, Nathaniel contented himself with allowing his gaze to rest on her, his mind filling with questions as regarded her behavior. What was she looking for? Was it a particular gentleman that had promised to be here this evening? He hoped that it was not some sort of assignation, for he would be honor-bound to intervene if such a thing was to occur, and he was not the sort of gentleman to do such a thing. Instead, he preferred to keep back from society as a whole, to remain fairly quiet and unobtrusive.

The young lady sighed heavily, and the sound caught his ears just as the music from the orchestra died away.

His heart began to grow heavy for her, wondering what it was that seemed to pain her so.

"You must do this," he heard her say, and before he could remove his gaze from her, the young lady turned back to the steps and moved out of the alcove—only to stumble back with a small shriek at the sight of him.

His heart dropped to the floor.

"I do apologize," he stammered, hurrying out of his alcove and moving towards her as she struggled to regain her balance. "I did not mean to startle you." Reaching out his hand, he waited for her to grasp it, not wanting to press himself forward more than he was doing. Thankfully, the young lady took a hold of it at once, and he was able to pull her gently out of the alcove and back to a steady stance. Breathing hard, he dropped his hand to his side and made to apologize again, only for a sudden realization to hit him hard, forcing his breath from his lungs.

It was Miss Bavidge.

"Miss Bavidge," he stammered, without thinking. "Good evening."

The young lady blinked rapidly, color rushing into her face. "Good evening," she replied, slowly, fanning herself with one hand as though to cool her reddened cheeks. "I do not think we have been introduced, *sir*." One eyebrow lifted slowly, a look of recognition coming into her eyes. "Although I do believe that I have seen you at some other events of late."

Nathaniel flushed, realizing too late that not only was this young lady particularly astute but that she was also unafraid of speaking to him in such a blunt manner. Yes, it was true that she had seen him at something prior to this evening—and it had not only been on one occasion but on a few. He had not thought that she had noticed his interest in her, but apparently, he had been wrong. However, a part of him was grateful at her lack of recognition. It meant that she had no knowledge of his part in her father's downfall only last season, and that, he hoped, would continue to be the case as the season continued.

"I—I believe we were introduced last season," he stammered, the lie coming quickly to his lips. "Or mayhap it was the season before that." The truth was, he had no knowledge as to whether or not Miss Bavidge had been in London two years ago, but he had needed to say something to give some explanation as to his interest in her. "I did not know whether or not you would recall."

It was Miss Bavidge's turn to look embarrassed, although Nathaniel felt a swell of guilt in his heart that he had made her so when the words from his mouth had been nothing more than a lie. It was too difficult to take such words back now, however, and so he had to continue as they were.

"I apologize that I do not recall your name nor your face, sir," Miss Bavidge replied quickly, her eyes darting from his. "Might you be good enough to introduce yourself to me again?"

He cleared his throat, trying to behave as gallantly as possible so as to cover his shame. "Viscount Morton, Miss Bavidge." He managed a small bow, although the space did not give him adequate room to perform one correctly. "Might I accompany you into the ballroom?" He held out his arm, hoping that their presence here together at the door to the ballroom had not been noticed by anyone. "We might then seek out your chaperone?"

Miss Bavidge's eyes narrowed, which took him completely by surprise. She did not accept his arm but walked down the three steps alone, turning to the left as she reached the ballroom and melting into the shadows. Nathaniel was left standing alone, not at all certain what had just occurred nor what he had done to offend the lady so. Unable to prevent himself from following her, he too descended quickly and then turned to the left just as she had done.

Miss Bavidge was not standing too far away, although she lingered in the shadows again, clearly trying to remain as unobtrusive as possible. Watching her for a moment or two longer, Nathaniel cleared his throat and then came towards her again, inclining his head as her attention was caught.

"I apologize if I have offended you, Miss Bavidge," he said, telling himself inwardly that he had no reason to worry over what she thought of him but finding it quite impossible to turn away from her. "I simply meant that—"

"I am aware that my presence here in London brings more than a few rumors and gossip whispers with it," Miss Bavidge interrupted, not looking at him but rather keeping her gaze out towards the crowd. "You need not suggest that I find my chaperone so as to keep those rumors at bay, Lord Morton, for I am certain that nothing I do and certainly nothing I say will prevent the *beau monde* from taking great pleasure in speaking about me."

"Indeed, that was not at all my intention when I said such a thing, Miss Bavidge," Nathaniel replied urgently, wanting to dissuade her of the notion that he gave any consideration to the rumors, such as they were. "It was merely because I thought the lady, whomever she might be, would be looking for you. Concerned, mayhap, as to where you had gone."

This did not seem to satisfy Miss Bavidge, for she looked at him sharply, her lips pulled tautly, and she took a step closer to him, coming a little more into the light. Nathaniel held her gaze steadily, taking her in and praying that she would believe him to be entirely honest, for he had truly not meant any offense by his suggestion.

In studying her, Nathaniel allowed himself to watch her closely, taking in everything about her. She was dressed in a rather plain gown of dark cream, with very little embellishments, and her fair hair was tied up with a few curls spilling down from the back of her head. The color of her gown did not lend itself to highlighting her golden head, for it was far too similar in tone. However, Nathaniel considered that he would not think her plain in any way, for her eyes, whilst still narrowed, were a comely shade of blue, framed by thick, dark lashes, and her oval face holding some delicate features. If she were not glaring at him so furiously, he might consider her to be quite pretty.

"Very well, Lord Morton," Miss Bavidge said finally, turning away from him and looking out across the crowd once more. "I shall accept your explanation but, whilst I appreciate your concern, I can assure you that there is none required. My...*chaperone*, as you so put it, has no consideration for me whatsoever. Therefore, you need not be troubled." A tight, pained smile caught her face, her eyes flicking to his for just a moment, although nothing more was said. Nathaniel felt his heart rip at the pain in her eyes, a pain that she was trying so hard to conceal through her fierce demeanor, yet still leaked through.

"Might you care to dance, Miss Bavidge?"

Quite where those words had come from, Nathaniel did not know, but he found himself inclining his head and extending one hand out towards Miss Bavidge before he could stop himself. Lifting his gaze to hers, he saw her blinking rapidly again, clearly a sign of astonishment, although she said nothing to him.

"I mean no harm to you," he assured her, wondering if she was ever going to take his hand or if he would be forced to drop it and step back in embarrassment. "Truly, Miss Bavidge, it would be my honor to dance with you."

Miss Bavidge tipped her head to the left just a little, regarding him carefully as though wondering whether or not he could be trusted. Nathaniel did not blame her. He had seen how she had been caught off guard by other gentlemen seeking to dance with her who had then, once the dance had come to a close, done nothing but whisper about her to their friends. It was as though it were some cruel trick, as though they wanted to give her hope only to dash it away again. Being amongst the gentlemen of the *ton* and frequenting Whites as often as he did, Nathaniel was all too aware of how Miss Bavidge's name was often thrust about in conversation, with many a gentleman asking whether or not another had danced with the 'daughter of the notorious scoundrel, Viscount Hawkridge.' It was almost a sense of pride that came with stating that yes, one had done so, and Nathaniel had hated to hear the coarse laughter that had followed. Some had even gone as far to suggest that Miss Bavidge would be so desperate for company, so longing for the interest of a gentleman that she could easily be cajoled into any sort of liaison that a gentleman wished to pursue —but thankfully, no one, as yet, had attempted to do such a thing.

Not that he thought Miss Bavidge would be as easy to encourage as the other gentlemen of the *beau monde* seemed to think, Nathaniel considered wryly, his hand still extended as the lady continued to study him. He was just about to give up and take a step back, only for the lady to sigh and place her hand in his—although she turned her head away as she did so, as though too ashamed of her behavior to look at their joined hands.

"I have been made a mockery of by almost every other gentleman present at some time or another over the last fortnight," she said heavily. "Therefore, what does it matter if I do so again?"

Nathaniel shook his head, pressing her fingers for a moment. "I am not such a gentleman, I assure you, Miss Bavidge," he replied, firmly, wanting to remove that consideration from her mind almost at once but knowing that it would be impossible to do so with only words. "Ah, a waltz begins, I see. Might you care for that?"

Miss Bavidge heaved a great sigh as though to suggest this was a great tribulation for her, but then nodded. "I can see no reason why not," she murmured, looking at him sidelong. "But be aware, Lord Morton, that you shall have a good many people watching you." She shrugged as he led her onto the floor. "But mayhap that is what you seek, despite your protestations otherwise."

Nathaniel said nothing, taking her onto the floor and bowing as he was supposed to. Miss Bavidge curtsied beautifully, although the expression on her face stated that she did not much care for either him or their dance. Nathaniel did not hold it against her, knowing that she had been ill-treated by the *ton* thus far, and finding himself feeling a tad guilty over his lies to her only a few minutes earlier. The music began, and he took her in his arms, seeing how she turned her head away from his, as though to keep as far apart from him as was possible in such a hold. As he began to move her about the floor, Nathaniel found that Miss Bavidge was as stiff as a board and did not soften in the least in his arms. She showed no enjoyment, did not speak even a word to him, and by the time the music ended, Nathaniel himself found himself relieved that it had come to an end.

"Thank you, Miss Bavidge," he murmured, bowing over her hand before letting it go completely. "I do hope that you will come to think better of me now when I prove that I am not as every other gentleman that you have come across thus far."

Miss Bavidge frowned, looking at him with a tinge of curiosity in her gaze as he let go of her hand. "I look forward to being proven wrong, Lord Morton," she told him, quickly turning away to make her way back to the side of the ballroom. "And thank you."

Nathaniel let her go from his side without wanting to call her back, finding that his frustration with her behavior towards him was tinged with guilt. The reason he had been watching Miss Bavidge since he had first noticed her back in society, the reason that he had danced with her to prove that he was not as any other gentleman of the *ton* was, he realized was merely to assuage his own guilt over the situation she was currently in. The blackening of her father's good name had been entirely Lord Hawkridge's fault, of course, but Nathaniel himself had been the one who had brought the incident and Lord Hawkridge's intention to light. Unfortunately, he had trusted one of his closest friends to keep such news to himself and not to spread it about London, but he had made a mistake in doing so, for his friend had immediately gone to Whites and crowed about it from the rooftops. Nathaniel had hoped that the news of Lord Hawkridge's downfall could be kept quiet, aware that the gentleman had an unmarried daughter, but instead the opposite had happened. In some ways, Nathaniel felt to blame for Miss Bavidge's damaged reputation, which was why he had been watching her closely over the last fortnight, wanting to see how society accepted her. Unfortunately, it had not gone particularly well, which, it seemed, Miss Bavidge herself was all too aware of.

"You have no need to continue trying to improve the situation," he told himself, firmly, walking in the opposite direction from Miss Bavidge. "You did nothing wrong. There is no reason for your guilt."

But, try as he might, such a feeling would not leave him. Even though he did not see Miss Bavidge for the rest of the evening, and even though he danced with many other young ladies, the feelings of guilt and regret continued to bury their way into his soul. Miss Bavidge had done nothing wrong and had committed no crime, and yet she bore the brunt of her father's poor behavior. Lord Hawkridge stayed away from London whilst she attempted to navigate through society, clearly seeking a match for herself. A match that might never occur, given just how little aid she was being given by her chaperone, whoever that was to be. His heart twisted again as he recalled just how bitterly Miss Bavidge had spoken of her chaperone, telling him outright that they cared nothing for her now that they saw just how blackened her reputation was.

Perhaps you should do something more for the girl.

Nathaniel shook his head, rubbing at his forehead with the back of his hand. Now he was being foolish. He had no reason to involve himself with Miss Bavidge, particularly if there was the danger of her realizing who he was and what role he had played in her father's downfall.

So why could he not remove her face from his mind?

CHAPTER THREE

"*My* goodness, is that...?"

Emma came to a sudden stop at the sight of her quarry, whom she had been unable to catch the attention of over the last few days. Lady Smithton was walking alone through St James' Park, her face tipped towards the sky without so much as a parasol in her hand to hide her face from the sunshine.

Much to Emma's embarrassment, Lady Smithton halted in her walk and looked directly at Emma and her companion, Miss Westerly, whom Emma had become only recently acquainted with.

"Is there something you wish to say to me?" Lady Smithton asked, a sharpness to her tone that had Emma's cheeks flaring hot. "I know that there is a rumor going around London about the passing of my husband, but I can assure you that such rumors do not influence me in the slightest. I am also aware that Lady Blakely has decided that I am rude and cold in my manner and so has been speaking of such things to anyone who will listen.

Nothing has affected me as yet. Therefore, you are welcome to tell whomever you wish that you have seen me and even spoken to me, if you wish it, but pray, desist your gawping!" She arched a brow, now looking from Miss Westerly to Emma and back again. "Not only it is unspeakably rude, but it is also entirely unladylike for two young ladies such as yourselves."

Utterly mortified that Lady Smithton had heard her whisper so loudly, Emma was about to apologize and, thereafter, turn on her heel and hurry away, only to recall just how desperate she was for any sort of aid. Whilst she had made a very poor first impression, she could not allow such an impression to stand, and nor could she allow this chance to pass without being open and honest with Lady Smithton about her hope that she might assist Emma with regaining her status somewhat within society.

"I must apologize profusely for my rudeness, Lady Smithton," she began, stammering in a most embarrassing way. "I... I should not have been staring, nor whispering in such an improper manner, but it is only that I find myself rather in awe of you."

She saw the look of surprise jump into Lady Smithton's eyes and felt her hopes begin to rise. Perhaps Lady Smithton would not simply turn away from her now that her apology was given. Throwing a quick glance towards her companion, Emma saw that Miss Westerly had chosen to sit down on a bench some distance away, apparently making it quite clear that Emma had been the one to whisper so rudely about Lady Smithton. Turning back, Emma looked directly into Lady Smithton's face, not wanting to give the impression that she was about to shirk from her improper behavior. Lady Smithton regarded her carefully, her expression a little quizzical.

"Might I inquire as to your name?" Lady Smithton asked, her tone a good deal less sharp than before. "We have not exactly been introduced, although you appear to be well acquainted with me."

"Forgive me," Emma said, hurriedly, passing a hand over her eyes for a moment as her embarrassment flared once again. "You are correct to state that I have not been introduced to you." A sharp laugh escaped her. "I am again proving my impropriety and my failings, am I not?"

This lighthearted comment did not seem to win the smiles nor the attention of Lady Smithton, who merely frowned and waited for Emma to continue. Fearing that she was failing almost entirely with her explanations as to why she had sought out Lady Smithton in the first place, Emma tried to explain again.

"You attended Lord Churston's ball last evening and were pointed out to me, Lady Smithton. I will admit, however, that I have heard the gossip and the whispers about you beforehand, but I have given them no consideration, I assure you." Biting her lip, she saw the slight flickering of Lady Smithton's eyes and felt as though she had made a mistake in even mentioning the rumors. Swallowing hard, her skin prickling with unease, she tried to find something more to say but felt her mouth go dry.

Lady Smithton cleared her throat. "Your name, if you please," she said again, although the words were not harsh or angry.

"Oh, of course." Emma scraped into a quick curtsy

again, unable to remember if she had done so already. "Do excuse me, Lady Smithton. I am Miss Emma Bavidge, daughter to Viscount Hawkridge."

"I see," Lady Smithton said, no recognition in her expression. "I confess that I do not know your name nor that of your father, Miss Bavidge. Ought I? I was only in London some two years ago, but still, that name does not come to me."

Heat climbed into Emma's cheeks, and she dropped her head. Of course, Lady Smithton might not know about Lord Hawkridge's disgrace, given that she would have been in the midst of her mourning at the time it had occurred. "You have not heard, I suppose," she stated, as unequivocally as she could. "I am a little surprised, for it has been on the lips of almost everyone I know."

Lady Smithton's face gathered into a frown. "I have only been in London for a fortnight or so, Miss Bavidge. I have not heard a good deal other than my own name being mentioned!" She gave Emma a wry smile, which Emma returned at once, hoping that this would not be the end of their conversation. "Pray, do tell me."

The awareness that she would now have to go into detail about what her father had done made Emma somewhat anxious. "Might we walk for a few minutes, Lady Smithton?" she asked, hoping that Lady Smithton would understand. "It can be a heavy burden, and walking does aid me somewhat."

Thankfully, Lady Smithton agreed at once, gesturing to the path in front of them. "You need not fear that I will turn from you, Miss Bavidge," she said, kindness in her voice and expression that brought a flare of hope to

Emma's heart. "Whatever it is that concerns you, it will not bring about my immediate judgment."

"You are very kind, my lady," Emma replied, truly grateful that Lady Smithton was able to give her such attention and glad that her risk of introducing herself to such a lady seemed to be working out "Not everyone is as kind as you, I fear. My father's disgrace has become my own."

All at once, Lady Smithton's expression changed. Anger caught her eyes, her mouth pulling into a firm line that spoke of great displeasure. "If this is what has been troubling you, Miss Bavidge, then be assured that you may speak openly in the knowledge that I will not berate you nor think you shameful in any way. If your father's disgrace is entirely his own doing, then I shall give you none of the blame nor consider your reputation stained beyond hope. Please." She gestured towards Emma again. "Tell me all that has occurred."

Setting her shoulders, Emma drew in a long breath and began to explain. There was a great deal of pain in talking about her father's behavior, for it was truly shameful and had brought a good deal of sorrow to the family as a whole. And yet, as she spoke, Emma found herself beginning to find each word easier and easier to speak, as though in doing so, she was unburdening her heart.

"My father, Viscount Hawkridge, has a penchant for gambling and the like," she began, aware of just how regretful she sounded. "I will not go into details, but he was worried for his fortune due to his many debts and came across something that he thought he might use to aid him with this trouble." Her breath hitched at this, knowing that she was about to reveal the horror of it to Lady Smithton. "In short, Lady Smithton, my father attempted to blackmail someone who held a greater position in society than he. This was discovered and revealed, and my father's disgrace was made known."

"And you, also, have been torn down with him," Lady Smithton finished, as Emma looked at her, seeing the anger still lingering in Lady Smithton's expression. "Even though you had nothing whatsoever to do with the matter. Is that not correct?"

Emma nodded, swallowing hard before she replied. "It is exactly as you say, Lady Smithton."

Sighing heavily, Lady Smithton shook her head, clearly displeased. "That is, I'm afraid, the woman's lot. We are often thrown together with our husbands, brothers, or fathers, to the point that their behavior and their rather foolish choices smear us with their disgrace. It seems quite unfair; do you not think?"

Emma looked up sharply, practically feeling the understanding growing between them. "Yes," she said at once, nodding fervently. "Yes, indeed I do. I have one or two close friends, and they treat me very well, I am glad to say."

This seemed to bring some sort of relief to Lady Smithton, for her shoulders settled back again, no longer rising high with tension. "Good," the lady said, firmly, although thereafter, nothing more was said. Emma walked in silence for a few moments, her awkwardness growing steadily as she tried to find a way to express what she hoped to gain by furthering her acquaintance with Lady Smithton.

"Lady Smithton," she began, her breath hitching as she struggled to speak clearly.

"Yes, Miss Bavidge?"

"Might I..." Emma trailed off, an expression of frustration rifling through her features. "Forgive me. What I ought to say is, if you are so willing, Lady Smithton, might I be permitted to call upon you one day soon? There is something more that I would like to discuss with you, if you would grant me a few minutes of your time."

Emma saw the way Lady Smithton hesitated, clearly thinking through what Emma had asked. It was little wonder that the lady was confused, for Emma had not only behaved poorly by whispering so loudly but had then gone on to introduce herself and then had somehow managed to beg an audience with Lady Smithton without any explanation as to why she wished to do so. To ask to call upon someone in such a manner was not considered polite, she knew, but her desperation was growing with each passing day. If she did not have Lady Smithton's help, then there would be very little hope for her to find a suitable husband. She would remain a spinster and have to spend her days with her father, who would, of course, continue to gamble whenever the opportunity was presented to him. Such a prospect was more than Emma could bear.

"Well, Miss Bavidge," Lady Smithton said, suddenly, breaking the silence. "I can see that there is something weighing heavily on your mind, therefore, I would be glad for you to call upon me." She smiled at Emma's obvious and apparent delight, holding up one hand before Emma could speak again. "You will tell me then why you think me so admirable, I hope?" she asked, her eyes twinkling. "After all, you are the first lady I have heard whispering about me, who then promises that they are somehow 'in awe' of me, although I cannot possibly imagine why!"

Emma laughed, her face lighting up as her hands pressed together to contain her relief and delight. This was more wonderful than she had ever thought, and the kindness of Lady Smithton was greater than she had hoped. "I shall, of course," she promised, eagerly. "I do speak the truth, Lady Smithton, I promise you."

"Then I think I would be very glad if you would call upon me, so that I might understand fully," Lady Smithton replied, her smile lingering. "Shall we say early next week?"

Emma nodded enthusiastically, wondering what Miss Crosby's reaction would be once she discovered that Emma had been successful in her endeavors. "That would be wonderful, Lady Smithton. I cannot thank you enough."

Lady Smithton nodded but gave her a small, wry smile. "I just hope that I am able to assist you with whatever it is you wish to discuss, Miss Bavidge."

"Oh, I am quite certain that you will be able to, Lady Smithton," Emma replied at once, brimming with confidence that Lady Smithton would be more than able to do so. "I must go. I can see that my friend is waiting for me." Again, she dropped into a curtsy, feeling that she could never find the words to express her full gratitude.

Tugging out her card from her reticule, she handed it to Lady Smithton with another small smile. "Here is my card, Lady Smithton. And thank you."

"You are most welcome," Lady Smithton replied, accepting the card and then turning away so that she might continue her walk in the park. Emma was breathless with joy as she returned to Miss Weatherly, who was looking at her agog, clearly desperate to know what it was Emily had been speaking to Lady Smithton about.

Emma, filled with relief and a sense of growing hope, grinned broadly at her friend as she rose to her feet to greet Emma again.

"I do not know what you thought you were doing, introducing yourself to Lady Smithton in such a fashion!" Miss Weatherly protested as Emma merely chuckled. "What was it that you spoke of? I could hardly believe it when you fell into step together for a short time, not after the awkwardness of our impropriety!"

Emma laughed softly and began to walk back towards the entrance of the park with Miss Weatherly walking alongside her. "I have had in mind that I wished to speak to Lady Smithton about a matter of particular importance but, having only seen her in person last evening, I have not had the opportunity to speak to her directly."

"But to do so without being introduced!" Miss Weatherly exclaimed, somewhat overawed by Emma's audacity. "That was rather bold, I must say."

"It has worked out well, however," Emma answered, thinking that the warm afternoon suddenly seemed a good deal brighter than before. "It seems that, in this case, taking a bold risk has paid off quite well."

As they made their way to the entrance of the park, Emily considered the other risk she had taken only last evening, when Lord Morton had asked her to dance with him. She had fully expected him to laugh and mock her thereafter, as so many of the other gentlemen had done, but much to her surprise, he had proved himself to be entirely truthful in his promise not to do so. He had merely faded into the crowd, dancing with other young ladies and never once frequenting groups of gentlemen in order to make it known that he too had danced with Miss Bavidge. A small smile caught the corner of her mouth as Miss Weatherly climbed into the waiting carriage, leaving Emma to follow thereafter. Lord Morton had been one short, bright moment in an otherwise dark evening and now, knowing that Lady Smithton was at the very least, willing to speak to her and listen to what she had to say, Emma felt as though this season might not turn out so terribly after all.

 ne week later

"And you think I could discover which gentlemen are suitable and then introduce you to them." Lady Smithton's eyes ran from Emma to her friend, Miss Crosby, and then back again. "I can see the hope that you have, Miss Bavidge, although I cannot be certain that I am the one who is best able to help you."

Emma knew that she had to be honest, aware that her friend Sarah was already battling her desperation and tears. "We have no other, Lady Smithton. There is no one within our own family to aid us, and certainly, none within the *ton* would be willing to do so. With the rumors and gossip surrounding my father, you know how I have been and will be treated by the majority of gentlemen. If you could only guide me in how to rise above such whispers and lead me to those gentlemen who might have a softer heart, then that would be the greatest of kind-nesses. Yet, I will understand completely if you do not wish to pursue matters with us. We do not know you, and you do not know us. I would not have any guilt in your heart over our situation. Whatever you decide, I am truly grateful that you were willing to listen to us both."

Her mouth went dry as Lady Smithton frowned and nodded, still looking from one to the next. Her hopes were either to crash to the ground or flare to the skies depending on what Lady Smithton decided. It felt like the most important moment of her life.

"Very well," Lady Smithton, after a moment, "but I must do a little more thinking on the matter before I decide *exactly* what will take place."

Emma could only nod, hearing Sarah gasp with astonishment and delight beside her, before pulling out her handkerchief to dab at her eyes. She did not know what to say; such was her gratitude as she began to battle tears. Lady Smithton was looking at them both with a small but gentle smile on her face, making Emma believe that they would soon become very dear friends.

"Thank you, Lady Smithton," she managed to say, her voice hoarse and breaking with emotion. "With all of my heart, I thank you. You do not know what you have done for us."

Lady Smithton smiled back at her, appearing quite contented with her decision. "But of course," she replied, warmly. "I am quite sure that very soon, I will see you both happy and settled. You need not struggle alone any longer."

Miss Crosby stifled a sob as Lady Smithton got up to

ring the bell for more tea. Emma reached across and pressed her friend's hand, aware that she could not speak but was overcome with thanks.

"A little more sustenance, I think," Lady Smithton said, sitting back down in her seat and offering Miss Crosby a warm and encouraging smile. "We shall become firm friends by the end of this afternoon, I am sure of it. Now, Miss Bavidge, why do we not begin with you? Tell me all you can about yourself."

Emma was not quite certain what to say, aware that she had told Lady Smithton the details of her father's gambling debts and the fact that her elder brother was married, settled, and entirely unwilling to come to her aid or involve himself in any way.

"I... I do not know what to say, Lady Smithton," she stammered, suddenly feeling a trifle awkward. "What is it you wish to know?"

Lady Smithton chuckled. "You must not consider yourself in the light of your father's behavior," she told Emma, warmly. "Tell me about yourself, what you enjoy, and what your preferences are." She leaned a little further forward. "And do be honest with me, Miss Bavidge, as to whether or not any particular gentlemen have caught your eye thus far."

Emma tried to laugh, but it came out as a mere croak as the image of Lord Morton rushed into her mind in a fury. "None," she stammered, her voice hoarse and rasping. "They have all, for the most part, treated me with very little consideration. Some dance with me and then go to speak of it to their companions, as though it is some sort of accolade to have shown me some attention. Others ignore me completely."

Lady Smithton nodded slowly, although her gaze lingered still, clearly waiting for Emma to say more. Emma, aware of the flush that was rising up her neck and into her cheeks, looked away and lifted one shoulder. "There has been one gentleman who has not treated me in either of the ways I have just described, however," she finished knowing that she had to be completely honest with Lady Smithton but finding it hard to speak nonchalantly. "He danced with me and seemed to show some true consideration for me, but thus far, he has been the only one."

Lady Smithton's smile began to spread wide across her face. "Then that is an excellent place to begin!" she said, encouragingly. "A gentleman who has shown that he can, in fact, behave appropriately. And he wanted to dance with you, you say?"

Emma nodded, surprised by her reaction to remembering just how Lord Morton had managed to prove himself to her. "He did. I accepted, fully believing him to go to his companions thereafter and mock me in some fashion or other, but to my surprise, he did not." Her voice grew a little wistful. "He told me he would not behave as the others had done, and whilst I did not immediately believe him, it turns out that he spoke the truth."

"Then I think it best we seek him out again," Lady Smithton said, as the door opened for the trays of tea and cakes to be brought in. "What was his name?"

Emma cleared her throat, pretending to try to recall even though she knew his name instantly. "Viscount

Morton," she said, after a few moments, desperately wanting to pretend that she had not even the smallest flicker of interest in the fellow. "I know nothing of him, of course, so I cannot tell whether or not—"

"Excellent!" Lady Smithton interrupted, her eyes flared with excitement. "I have a friend that I may call upon in order to determine the truth about your Lord Morton, Miss Bavidge, but for the time being, shall we hope that you might be able to further your acquaintance with this gentleman? If he is as honest and as well-mannered as you have described, then at the very least, his acquaintance is worth pursuing." She hesitated, her smile fading as she looked at Emma and then turned her gaze to Miss Crosby, who had finally finished crying.

"I must ask you both," Lady Smithton began, the excitement gone from her voice completely. "Do you wish for love?"

Emma frowned at this, glancing across at Miss Crosby and seeing her shake her head fervently.

"No," Miss Crosby said, stoutly. "I shall be glad of a decent gentleman who will treat me kindly, that is all. I have no need for love."

"Nor I," Emma replied, quickly, knowing that she was foolish even to let herself think of such a thing. "I know that most matches within society come from suitability of title and the like, and, like Miss Crosby, I seek only a contented future with a gentleman who will be considerate and kind."

This appeared to satisfy Lady Smithton, who nodded and smiled, reaching out to pour the tea. "That is a relief, I must admit," the lady replied, as she filled the cups.

"Love between husband and wife might bloom once the marriage has taken place, but it would be more than difficult to engage you both in a marriage of love." She smiled at Emma as she handed her the delicate china saucer and the small teacup placed atop it. "Although if you are blessed with such a thing, then you are to be considered very lucky."

Emma laughed and shook her head in mock dismay. "I have found no luck in my life thus far, Lady Smithton," she told her. "Therefore, I highly doubt that something as wonderful as that might occur in my life. I shall be content to find a suitable gentleman and shall not ask for more."

Lady Smithton nodded, considering this for a moment or two. "Then you are very wise," she replied firmly. "Very wise indeed. Have no fear, Miss Crosby, Miss Bavidge. We shall work together to ensure that you are both married and settled just as soon as can be. And we shall start tomorrow."

The following evening found Lydia standing in her usual place at the side of the room whilst the music and the dancing swirled about in front of her. Almacks was busy this evening, which came as no surprise, but Lady Smithton had managed to ensure that she and her aunt were present this evening and, of course, her aunt could not have refused to attend something such as this! Miss Crosby would be here too, no doubt, although as yet, Emma had not seen her.

Your one intention is to speak to Lord Morton again.

Emma's skin prickled as she looked all about her, wondering if Lord Morton would even be present this evening. She did not know where to look for him, recalling how he had been skulking back in an alcove the first time she had met him, although it had not been the first time she had seen him watching her.

A flush of heat ran through her as she recalled those dark blue eyes of his, remembering how they had held her gaze steadily before dropping to run down her frame. A slight shudder caught her, forcing her to think clearly. She could not allow herself to be so caught up by the thought of a mere gentleman simply because he had been kind to her. That meant nothing. A kind gentleman might simply be kind but have no willingness to further his acquaintance with her and she ought not to expect that Lord Morton would be so amiable to the idea. After all, she still carried the disgrace of her father's behavior with her wherever she went so any gentleman who showed her any interest whatsoever would have to bear the gossip and the whispers that came with courting her.

Her stomach turned over, and she closed her eyes, trying to force back the sudden, overwhelming fear that no gentleman would wish to do such a thing. She had hope now, did she not? Lady Smithton had agreed to help her, and so, therefore, Emma was no longer alone in her struggle to work her way through the tangled web that made up high society. She sighed heavily and slumped back against the wall, her eyes still closed tightly.

"Miss...Bavidge?"

The hesitant words made her eyes fly open, a furious

blush coursing through her cheeks as she looked up to see none other than the gentleman she had been thinking of looking down at her, his expression somewhat uncertain.

"Lord Morton," she stammered, unsure what she should say or whether she should give some sort of explanation for her behavior. "I was simply thinking about something of great importance."

Lord Morton gave her a half smile, blinking quickly. "I see," he said as if this was a simple enough explanation for her closed eyes and heavy sigh that he had, no doubt, heard. "It is good to see you again this evening."

Emma was robbed of speech for a moment, finding it difficult to know what it was that she should say to such a compliment. Was he being truthful? Was he truly glad to see her here again?

"I believe I owe you an apology, Lord Morton," she said, remembering what had occurred the last time they had spoken. Seeing his quizzical look, she dropped her eyes to the ground, embarrassed. "You told me you were not like the other gentlemen of my acquaintance, and I did not immediately believe you."

"Oh." Lord Morton chuckled softly, and immediately, some of Emma's embarrassment began to fade. "That is quite all right, Miss Bavidge. I can well understand your reasoning behind believing that I was not what I said. You need not apologize to me for that."

"You are very good, Lord Morton," Emma replied, aware that her face was still hot with embarrassment. "I thank you for your understanding."

Silence lingered between them for a moment or two, leaving Emma uncertain as to what to say next. Her mouth went dry as she struggled to consider what should come next in their conversation, wondering if Lord Morton had deliberately sought her out or if he had been sent by Lady Smithton, who was, certainly, present already.

"Do you know Lady Smithton?"

Emma's head lifted sharply as she spoke, just as Lord Morton said, "Would you care to dance this evening?"

They both looked at one another for a moment or two, wide-eyed, until finally, Lord Morton began to laugh, appearing a trifle more relaxed than before. Emma let her lips curve into a smile, studying Lord Morton and finding that his entire expression changed when he laughed. His dark brown hair, neat and tidy, jostled violently, his eyes gleaming with good humor. There seemed to be an ease of manner about him now, the confusion between them dying away quickly as the atmosphere changed.

"I do apologize, Miss Bavidge," Lord Morton said, still grinning at her. "What was it you wished to ask me?"

Emma forgot for a moment, before recalling that she wished to speak to him about Lady Smithton. "I wondered if you knew Lady Smithton," she replied, pressing her hands together in front of her. "She has recently become a close acquaintance of mine and I—"

"Lady Smithton?" Lord Morton interrupted, his smile fading and a slight frown forming between his brows. "Is she not the one who supposedly killed her husband?"

Stiffening, Emma lifted her chin a notch, feeling a rush of hot anger course through her veins. "I did not think that you gave a good deal of sway to rumors, Lord Morton," she said, tightly. "Surely you must know that this is nothing more than idle gossip!"

Lord Morton turned his head away, but not before Emma saw a slight redness to his cheek.

"You are quite correct, of course," Lord Morton said, after a beat of silence. "Those are rumors, and I have made it my sole intention to refuse to listen to such things. As I have done with you, Miss Bavidge."

This was meant to encourage her, Emma knew, but there was still something of her anger left. Perhaps Lord Morton was not as infallible as she had first thought.

"If you will permit me to ask my question now, Miss Bavidge," Lord Morton continued, quickly. "Might you care to dance with me this evening? Or is your dance card quite full?"

Emma shook her head, surprised to see the flare of disappointment that jumped into Lord Morton's eyes. "I am not engaged to a single gentleman this evening," she replied, ignoring the kick of sadness that came with such a statement. "As such, Lord Morton, you may have your choice of dances."

Lord Morton seemed to slump with relief, reaching out for her dance card and jotting his name down in not one but two dances. Emma watched him cautiously, wondering at his reaction. Had he been disappointed because he thought she would refuse him? Surely not!

"Excellent," Lord Morton said, his voice a little louder than before. "I look forward to standing up with you, Miss Bavidge."

"Thank you, Lord Morton," Emma replied, as he

gave her a small bow, preparing to take his leave. "I look forward to it also."

As Lord Morton left her side, Emma could not help but allow her gaze to linger on him. He was handsome and seemingly very kind, but there was still so much about him that she did not know. She certainly would not allow her heart to become engaged with his, not when she did not know the fellow in any particular way. Yes, he had been honest and truthful with her, seemingly determined not to allow the gossip that surrounded her to affect him in any way, but it was much too soon to consider him a potential suitor. She knew very little about him, although Emma had to admit that there was a warm glow in her heart as she looked down at her dance card and saw his name there.

"Lord Morton, I believe?"

Emma looked up to see Lady Smithton coming near to her, turning her head to look at the departing gentleman.

"Yes, that was he," Emma replied, with a small smile. "I have his name secured for two dances."

Lady Smithton seemed delighted at this. "Quite wonderful," she exclaimed, beaming at Emma. "And I am certain you shall have a few more very soon." She turned and began to move away, turning her head to hurry Emma along after her. "Do join me, Miss Bavidge. I have some acquaintances I wish to introduce you to."

"At once," Emma replied, hurrying after her friend, who was almost entirely swallowed up by the crowd of guests that swarmed all about her. Moving quickly, she soon caught up with Lady Smithton, feeling her heart race wildly in her chest. A trifle anxious about being introduced and fearing that one or two might either give her the cut direct or merely watch her with an amused look on their faces, Emma tried to set her shoulders and walk as tall as she could. The *beau monde* did not need to see her pain and suffering at their hands. She had to remain above it.

"Have no fear, Miss Bavidge," Lady Smithton said, encouragingly, as though she could see into Emma's heart and know what she was feeling. "No one will dare treat you ill, I promise."

"I must hope so," Emma replied, tightly, her stomach now in knots as a group of gentlemen and ladies turned as one to look at both herself and Lady Smithton as they approached.

Lady Smithton laughed and linked arms with Emma. "I am certain of it," she replied, with a broad smile. "You will find that there is more than one gentleman akin to Lord Morton, Miss Bavidge. Who knows? You might even discover that you have a few gentlemen eager to court you!"

But none shall make such an imprint on my mind as Lord Morton has done, Emma thought to herself, forcing a smile to her lips as she drew near. Lord Morton had been the one to seek her out, to come to her on now two separate occasions, as though he were truly interested in her acquaintance, and that was something Emma was certain she would never be able to forget.

CHAPTER FIVE

"*D*id I not see you dancing with Miss Bavidge last evening?"

Nathaniel tensed visibly, a sheet of anger draping itself over him. He knew that voice all too well.

"Come now," the gentleman continued, setting down two glasses of whisky before settling himself in the chair opposite Nathaniel. "You can tell me the truth of it, can you not?" He grinned broadly, but Nathaniel only felt his fury grow steadily. "We were once very good friends."

"That was before you betrayed my confidence," Nathaniel replied tightly, his hands clenching into fists. "You know I have no wish to speak to you, Rochester."

Viscount Rochester had once been a close friend of Nathaniel's. They had enjoyed good conversation, fine brandy, and making eyes at any young debutante that should happen to pass in front of them—although Lord Rochester always sought to pursue such young ladies with a good deal more fervency that Nathaniel ever allowed himself to do. That had been one side of his friend that he had not appreciated, although he had always merely shrugged and silently considered that a gentleman had to make his own decisions about his behavior.

However, when the difficulties with Lord Hawkridge had been revealed, Nathaniel had needed someone to talk to, someone to share his burden with. His first thought had been to speak to his longtime friend, trusting that nothing would be shared once Nathaniel had told him the truth. Lord Rochester had even agreed to remain entirely silent about whatever Nathaniel told him, and so Nathaniel had unburdened himself completely.

Unfortunately, Lord Rochester had proven himself not to be a man of his word. Finding the gossip much too enticing to keep to himself, he had gone out and spoken to everyone he wished about this news. And so had been the end of Lord Hawkridge within London society.

And with Lord Hawkridge's swift and ashamed exit from London had gone his daughter, Miss Bavidge. Even now, the thought of what she must have had to endure bit at his soul, knowing just how difficult it was for her at this present moment to even go about society.

"You are being quite foolish, Lord Morton," Lord Rochester stated, sighing heavily and waving a hand in Nathaniel's direction. "You did the right thing in revealing Lord Hawkridge's actions."

"But it was never my intention to make it fodder for the rumor mills!" Nathaniel protested loudly, leaning forward in his chair and fixing his acquaintance with a hard stare. "I trusted you to keep such matters to yourself, and you did not."

Lord Rochester said nothing for a moment or two before sighing heavily again and flopping back in his seat, one hand holding loosely onto his brandy as it sloshed about in the bottom of the glass.

"You are much too sensitive, Morton," Lord Rochester said, eventually, rolling his eyes as though Nathaniel was behaving ridiculously. "There is no harm done by revealing the truth!"

"There was, and there is!" Nathaniel exclaimed, aware that his voice was echoing around Whites and drawing the attention of others but finding that he could not prevent himself from speaking so. "You knew full well that when you decided to share such intimate matters with your many, *many* acquaintances that Lord Hawkridge would have to depart from London in shame and mortification."

"Which is precisely what he deserved," Lord Rochester interrupted, his thick brows burrowing low over his eyes. "He had intentions to blackmail the Earl of Knighton, as you well know."

Nathaniel closed his eyes and forced himself to take two long breaths before he responded. "That is true, of course," he agreed, remembering how he had stumbled across Lord Hawkridge talking in low tones to another fellow and how he had been horrified to hear of the gentleman's intentions. He felt as much repugnance for Lord Hawkridge's behavior now as he had then and certainly did not regret his actions in bringing Lord Hawkridge's intentions to light—but he had done so in a way that should have kept the matter fairly quiet. The Earl of Knighton himself had been eager to do so, for then the question about what Lord Hawkridge had found would be kept silent, but it had gone entirely awry thanks to Nathaniel's decision to talk to his friend and, thereafter, Lord Rochester's decision to share such news with anyone who wanted to listen.

"Then why are you so upset about a few pieces of gossip?" Lord Rochester asked, sounding exasperated, "especially when the gentleman in question was forced to leave society and return home."

"Because," Nathaniel replied firmly, opening his eyes and looking directly into the face of Lord Rochester. "Because it was not only he who had to return home in disgrace. You may recall, Rochester, that the gentleman has a daughter." He saw Lord Rochester's expression change from exasperation to a sudden interest, his eyes widening slightly.

"I see," Lord Rochester murmured, sitting up a little straighter in his chair and looking directly back at Nathaniel. "So it is the young lady that you worry about."

Seeing the potential difficulty that could arise from such a confession, Nathaniel tried to avoid answering. "The Earl of Knighton was also left to bear the brunt of idle gossip," he told Lord Rochester, his voice grave. "The man wanted to keep the affair as quiet as he could so that no questions would be asked, so that no one would wonder what Lord Hawkridge had found. And then, because of your idle tongue, he had to defend himself from all manner of questions!"

Lord Rochester shrugged, a gleam in his eyes as he continued to watch Nathaniel. Nathaniel held his gaze firmly, although he had the uncomfortable feeling that

Lord Rochester was beginning to become aware of the source of Nathaniel's frustration towards him.

"Lord Knighton, from what I recall, is doing rather well for himself, however," Lord Rochester said, slowly, taking a quick sip of his brandy before continuing. "He is to be wed, is he not?"

Nathaniel shrugged, reaching for the glass of brandy on the table with some reluctance. He did not want to drink it, given that Lord Rochester had brought it for him, but at the same time felt as though he required some sustenance. "I do not know."

"Then you are not particularly concerned over Lord Knighton ," Lord Rochester chuckled, his eyes glinting in a somewhat malicious fashion. "You are concerned for Miss Bavidge. Is that not her name?"

Nathaniel flinched at the sound of Miss Bavidge's name on Lord Rochester's lips. "My quarrel is with you, Rochester," he said, again trying to avoid the question. "I trusted you, and you betrayed that."

"Tosh!" Lord Rochester laughed, drawing the attention of yet more patrons. "You are upset on the behalf of Miss Bavidge, are you not?" Nathaniel made to protest, made to state quite clearly that he had been saddened by his friend's unwillingness to keep his word, but Lord Rochester was not about to listen to him. "You have seen Miss Bavidge back amongst us, have seen how little her aunt cares for her, and your heart has been unable to remove the guilt that has lingered within ever since you first spoke to the Earl of Knighton last season." Lord Rochester chuckled horribly, his lip curling. "*That* is what upsets you, what angers you, Morton," he finished, sitting back in his seat with a satisfied expression. "You wanted to protect Miss Bavidge from the consequences of her father's actions, but you have been unable to." He shook his head, his laughter now changed to a sneer. "You have always been too soft hearted."

Nathaniel swallowed hard, feeling as though his throat were closing tightly as his hands curled into fists. A few other gentlemen had drawn near to them both, clearly listening to everything that was being said whilst flickers of interest showed in their expressions. He did not know what to say. The truth was that he had sought to do as the Earl of Knighton had asked in keeping the matter as quiet as he could whilst ensuring that Lord Hawkridge was not allowed to continue behaving in such a manner. The intention had been to ask Lord Hawkridge to call upon him and, when the gentleman arrived, both Nathaniel and Lord Knighton would have been present. They would have presented what they knew of Lord Hawkridge's intentions to the gentleman, secure in the knowledge that the threat of revealing his poor behavior to the *ton* would ensure he stopped such activities at once. That would have sent the gentleman back to his estate, of course, but would also have protected the gentleman's daughter from disgrace whilst ensuring that Lord Knighton's secret remained precisely that. However, the matter had laid heavy on Nathaniel's mind, and so he had chosen to speak of it to someone he trusted. Little wonder that he had been so upset and so angry to discover that everything he had planned had been shattered in a single moment, and all at Lord Rochester's hand.

"I know," Lord Rochester continued when Nathaniel could think of nothing to say. "I shall court the young lady."

A hard fist slammed into Nathaniel's heart. "No," he said angrily. "You have made enough trouble already, Rochester."

Lord Rochester arched one eyebrow whilst a murmur ran around the assembled gentlemen who now held court.

"I did not think that you would protest, Morton," Lord Rochester replied, mildly, looking surprised. "Surely, if you are that concerned for Miss Bavidge's wellbeing, you would be glad to have someone such as myself court her."

Nathaniel set his jaw. "No, I would not," he stated, as firmly as he could. "You forget that I know of your reputation, Rochester."

Another murmur from the other gentlemen. Apparently, they too knew that Lord Rochester delighted in the company of young ladies and that he often pressed his attentions upon them a little too firmly.

Lord Rochester, however, merely shrugged. "Mayhap it is time for me to consider taking a wife," he replied evenly, his eyes narrowing slightly. "And might this not make up in some way for what I have done regarding my past behavior?" He smiled softly, throwing up a challenge into Nathaniel's face. "I confess I do not know the chit and certainly have not laid eyes on her—but even if I should court her for a time, that would bring her into society a little more, would it not?" He threw back the rest of his brandy and then chuckled. "Although I might change my mind and decide to marry such a creature. For surely, she will be so grateful for any sort of attention that she will be a biddable and easy wife, who will look aside when I pursue...other matters of interest."

Nathaniel felt as though he were about to explode with anger, his blood roaring in his ears and his heart thumping so loudly he was certain everyone could hear it. It seemed that Lord Rochester's intention was to marry and then continue living as though he were a bachelor, seeking out the company and companionship of anyone he chose. That could not be an acceptable life for any young lady and particularly not for someone such as Miss Bavidge, who had been through so much difficulty already! But Lord Rochester was correct in one regard, Nathaniel had to admit. Miss Bavidge might easily accept Lord Rochester's attentions since she had very few other considerations from the gentlemen of the *ton*.

"You could go and pursue her yourself, could you not?"

Nathaniel narrowed his eyes, his jaw working furiously.

"Ah, but of course you could not," Lord Rochester continued, leaning forward in his seat, his voice soft with apparent understanding. "You could not court the young lady whose father you so brutally threw from society."

"But I have seen Lord Morton dancing with Miss Bavidge on a few occasions," said one of the gentlemen standing nearby. "Surely then—"

Lord Rochester held up one hand, silencing the gentleman. He began to laugh softly, his eyes never leaving Nathaniel's. Nathaniel felt his stomach twist into a tight knot, aware now that Lord Rochester understood precisely what Nathaniel's difficulty was.

"Ah, so the truth of it is finally made known," Lord Rochester murmured, his expression dark and malevolent. "She does not know that it was you who discovered the intentions of her father. She is unaware that you were the one to bring it to the Earl of Knighton's attention." He tilted his head, looking almost thoughtful. "Does that mean, then, that she could be led to believe that you were the one who made everyone in society aware of Lord Hawkridge's disgrace?"

His breath tore from his lungs as Nathaniel realized what Lord Rochester was suggesting. He stared at his acquaintance, wondering just how he could ever have been friends with such a cruel, heartless gentleman such as this. Had Lord Rochester always been so calculating? So harsh and foreboding? He did not remember ever seeing such behavior from his once-friend before, but perhaps Lord Rochester had simply been good at hiding such things from him.

"What are you trying to do, Rochester?" he asked, his voice a trifle unsteady, such was his ire. "Why do you even suggest such a thing?"

Lord Rochester's lip curled all the more. "Because you have turned from me and heaped blame onto my shoulders," he replied, anger spiking his words. "You remove your friendship from me simply because of something I said, leaving the *beau monde* completely aware of what you thought of me and my actions. I will not accept such callous treatment, Morton."

Nathaniel closed his eyes, swallowing the painful

lump in his throat. He had not been silent when it had come to telling those he knew that Lord Rochester was nothing more than a gossip and a breaker of his trust, but he had never once suspected that his friend intended to punish him for such a thing! Now, it seemed, Lord Rochester had merely been biding his time, trying to find something or someone to use in order to punish Nathaniel—and he had managed to find something that would tear Nathaniel's heart apart with both guilt and the agony of being unable to tell Miss Bavidge the truth.

"Therefore, you can expect me to begin to court Miss Bavidge very soon," Lord Rochester continued, softly, lifting his glass and waving it at a nearby footman, who came to collect it at once. "I doubt that you will find the courage to tell her my intentions, for if you do so, then you will have to reveal all to her—and what will she think of you then?" He laughed horribly and rose from his chair. "And if you try to warn her away from me, then I might have to speak to her of what I know of you." The threat was clear. "You try to protect her as much as you try to protect yourself, Morton. There is no good in that, I assure you."

He walked away from Nathaniel, leaving him sitting in his chair with the glass of brandy frozen in his hand. Nathaniel did not know what to say or what to do, staring blankly ahead as he tried to find some way out of what Lord Rochester had threatened. All about him, the crowd of gentlemen began to talk in hushed tones, their words buzzing about Nathaniel's head like flies. A great chasm seemed to open up in front of him, leaving him feeling as though he were about to topple headlong into it, with no way to prevent himself from doing so. To protect Miss Bavidge from Lord Rochester would be to tell her the truth about what he had done to involve himself with her father's situation. Most likely, he would have to confess that he had told Lord Rochester of what had occurred, which had then led to Rochester himself spreading the gossip throughout London. He could imagine how she would react to such news, aware that there would be upset, anger and even hatred towards him for what he had done—not in preventing Lord Hawkridge from blackmailing Lord Knighton, but in speaking to Rochester and therefore, starting the very beginnings of the gossip that now surrounded her.

But to remain silent, to remain afar from her, would mean that Rochester would do his level best to encourage her affections and, most likely, Miss Bavidge would give them willingly. After all, that was why she had returned to London for the season, was it not? She had come to seek a match, as did most of the other young ladies who attended London. Being a little older meant that she had more urgency than most, and he did not think that she would be too specific about the sort of gentleman she required. Therefore, Lord Rochester had an excellent chance to succeed in his plan.

"I have to stop this," Nathaniel muttered to himself as a vision of Miss Bavidge floated before his eyes. She had seemed so brittle on the first occasion he had spoken to her, but it was a hardness that came from an attempt to hide her vulnerability. He had found himself seeking her out whenever he attended any social occasion, and on the times he had found her, he had sought to encourage her with a dance or two. That had only happened on two prior occasions, but it had been enough to convince him that Miss Bavidge was an intelligent, delightful young lady who had more than enough worth of her own to be considered as a bride for some suitable gentleman. He had just never even considered the possibility of courtship given that he would have to confess all should that occurred.

But now that Lord Rochester had made his intentions clear, Nathaniel felt his heart wrench in his chest. He wanted to do something, wanted to stop Lord Rochester in any way he could, but the only way that was open to him was barred by his own unwillingness. He did not want Miss Bavidge to hate him, but nor did he want Lord Rochester to succeed.

Just what was he to do?

CHAPTER SIX

"'*The* Spinster's Guild,' then."

Emma looked up from where she had been studying her dance card, seeing the gentleman that Lady Smithton had introduced only earlier that day.

"Good evening, Lord Havisham," she replied with a quick smile. "I see Lady Smithton has managed to convince you to come to our aid."

Lord Havisham allowed himself a long, pained sigh, giving her a roll of his eyes, which made her smile all the more. "Indeed, I have been convinced," he replied with a wry grin. "Lady Smithton is a very dear friend of mine, and I do not think I could refuse her anything. Besides which, I must prove myself to her, Miss Bavidge, and I intend not to allow myself to fail in any way."

Emma considered this, looking up at the gentleman's handsome face and wondering just how fond he was of Lady Smithton for his firm, and frankly, fairly vulnerable words had taken her by surprise. Lady Smithton had blushed just a little as she had introduced him to Emma, to Miss Crosby, and to the two other young ladies that had come to join them—Lady Amelia and Lady Beatrice —and that itself had caught Emma's attention. She had heard Lady Smithton state with some determination that she was not about to throw her heart to any other gentleman after what she had endured with her first husband, but it did not appear as though she was entirely immune to Lord Havisham's charms.

"Now, it seems that I am to give you guidance as to which gentlemen are suitable and which would be best avoided," Lord Havisham continued, looking a trifle uncomfortable as though he were not quite certain he could do the job that had been asked of him. "I will admit that I have the measure of most of the gentlemen within society, and it will be fairly easy to discover the truth about those I do not know." He gave her a half shrug. "Lady Smithton says that Lord Morton has been favoring you."

Emma blushed furiously and waved a hand. "He is not *favoring* me, no," she replied, trying not to allow such a statement to bother her. "He has been very kind and, from what I have seen of him, I believe him to have integrity and a strong character. He does not try to mock me as so many others have done. Instead, he seeks me out and dances with me upon occasion, so that I am not standing alone all evening."

Lord Havisham nodded slowly. Something flickered in his eyes—was it a question? A question over her or about Lord Morton? Emma was about to ask when Lord Havisham let out a long breath, frowned, and turned towards the rest of the guests.

"You have an aunt, I believe."

"Yes," Emma replied, her blush now turning to embarrassment. "I do not believe she ever truly wished to help me this season, although she did agree to do so with my father's cajoling. However, once we came to London and she realized that the gossip about my father's blackmail was still on everyone's lips, she has done all she can to remove herself from my side whenever we are in company. At home, she speaks to me quite as usual, but out of our townhouse, it is as though she is a stranger." Emma lifted one shoulder with a small shrug. "But what can I do? I could try to talk to her, to point out what a hypocrite she is being, but I know full well that she will not listen to me. Nor will anything I say make her change her behavior."

"Which is why you sought out Lady Smithton."

"Precisely," Emma agreed, smiling. "And so, 'The Spinsters Guild' has been formed!" She chuckled at the name that Lady Smithton had thrust upon the group earlier that afternoon. "Although the name in itself is fairly ironic, given that we are all attempting to avoid such a title!"

Lord Havisham chuckled along with her. "I am quite certain that Lady Smithton will guide you all towards success," he assured her, making Emma's smile grow. "Now, should you care to dance, Miss Bavidge?" He reached for her dance card and smiled at the name written there already. "Although I see Lord Morton has reached you before I. Nevertheless, I shall take two dances and, thereafter, should any gentleman wish to dance with you also, I shall be nearby to either encourage or dissuade you."

Smiling happily, Emma accepted his proffered arm, thinking to herself that this evening was, as far as she was concerned, going to be one of the best evenings she had enjoyed thus far since coming to London for the season. "Thank you, Lord Havisham," she answered as he began to lead her to the floor. "I am truly grateful for all of your help."

Once the dance was over, Lord Havisham led Emma towards a small cluster of guests who were standing together. He obviously knew some of them, for they turned to greet him the moment he stepped near to them, whilst some of the ladies eyed him with obvious and apparent interest. This did not surprise Emma, who knew that Lord Havisham was a handsome gentleman with both a title and a fortune. The gaze of the ladies then turned towards her, and Emma was surprised to see that one lady narrowed her eyes at her a little, making her somewhat uncomfortable.

"Might I present Miss Emma Bavidge," Lord Havisham said to the assembled guests. "She is a dear friend of Lady Smithton, and therefore, has become a friend of mine also."

This did not seem to please the ladies in question, who, although they all greeted her and dipped into curtsies, did not smile nor look at all happy to see her in the company of Lord Havisham.

"Miss Bavidge," one of the gentlemen said, flicking a

look of curiosity towards Lord Havisham, making Emma aware that this gentleman clearly knew of who she was and what her father had done. "How good to meet you. Lord Denver, at your service." He smiled and bowed, his brown hair flopping over his forehead as he did so.

Emma bobbed a curtsy, her tongue sticking to the roof of her mouth as she tried to murmur a greeting. Heat was climbing into her face as she silently prayed that Lord Havisham had not made a mistake by introducing her to such a fellow.

"Should you care for a dance, Miss Bavidge?" Lord Denver continued as Lord Havisham stepped away to speak to another acquaintance. "I would be glad to take you to the floor."

Emma hesitated, not stretching out her hand to give him her dance card as he obviously expected. "I... I am not certain that I—"

"You can trust Lord Denver," said a voice in her ear, making Emma jump in surprise. "He is a good sort." The voice came from a tall, broad-shouldered man who had dark green eyes and thick brown hair that seemed almost black in the candlelight. Emma did not think that they had ever been introduced, and yet to speak to her in such a knowing, and apparently friendly, fashion made her question whether or not she had simply forgotten their first meeting.

"Lord Rochester," the gentleman said with a small inclination of his head. "We were introduced last season."

Emma wanted to close her eyes and sink to the floor with the shame of not recalling this particular gentleman, but instead simply pasted a smile on her face and tried to make light of the situation. "Yes, of course," she replied quickly. "You must forgive me, Lord Rochester. It is just that I have been introduced to so many new acquaintances only a few minutes ago that I have quite lost my senses!"

Much to her relief, he chuckled and inclined his head again. "Then you need have no doubt that I shall not hold it against you," he replied, warmly. "I must say, I am sorry for the trouble you have found yourself in this season, Miss Bavidge. Those gentlemen who treat you so cruelly and the ladies whose tongues work faster than the flowing river should all be thoroughly ashamed of themselves."

This was said with such fervency that, for a moment, Emma found herself quite caught up with his determination, only to recall that she did not know anything about this gentleman aside from the fact that she had apparently been introduced to him last season. Wary as ever, she gave Lord Rochester a brief smile and then turned her attention back to Lord Denver. "I should be glad to dance with you, Lord Denver," she said, suddenly decisive. After all, if she were not to risk anything, then she would not make any progress! "Here." She held out her dance card, and Lord Denver took it at once, shooting Lord Rochester a quick grin. This made Emma somewhat uncomfortable, not certain as to whether this was a grin of triumph or one of amusement at Lord Rochester having been given so quick a brush off by Emma. Lord Rochester, however, appeared quite determined to capture her attention also, and so took another small step forward just as Lord Denver let the dance card drop.

"Might I also persuade you to accept my invitation to

dance?" he asked her, enquiringly. "I would be greatly honored if you would allow me to do so."

Emma did not know whether to accept him or not, glancing over Lord Rochester's left shoulder and noticing that Lord Havisham had his back to her, deep in conversation with someone other than she. Apparently, he had considered her quite safe with Lord Denver and therefore had presumed that she was continuing to converse with him. He had not seen Lord Rochester approach and, therefore, could give her no guidance as to whether or not she should accept him.

"I mean you no ill, Miss Bavidge," Lord Rochester continued, evidently seeing her hesitation. "Although I can understand your wariness."

Desperate, Emma looked at Lord Denver, who appeared to be frowning slightly as he regarded Lord Rochester. This could be no indication of Lord Rochester's character, however, for Lord Denver might merely dislike the fact that Lord Rochester had stepped in after him instead of allowing him a few minutes to talk with Emma alone.

"Very well," she said, eventually, feeling the air grow thick about her as tension began to rise between both herself and Lord Rochester. "But just one dance, if you please." A trifle reluctantly, she handed him her card and saw just how eagerly he grasped it. Scanning it quickly, he chuckled over something or other, something Emma had very little idea about, before writing his name down for the cotillion.

"I think this will do very well," he said, letting the

card drop and inclining his head as he did so. "A cotillion, Miss Bavidge. What say you to that?"

It is better than a waltz, Emma thought silently, aware that in a dance such as the cotillion, it was easier to speak to other dancers throughout instead of being able to speak only to one's partner. "Thank you, Lord Rochester," she murmured, aware that he was waiting for her answer. "You are very kind."

He did not answer but inclined his head, smiled, and then turned about on his heel to walk away. Emma let her eyes trail after him, fearing that he would turn around and find her staring at him but still feeling the need to watch his every moment in case he should display some sort of ill will towards her. To her surprise, he simply went to speak to another young lady, who appeared glad to see him. Her eyes lingered on him as he took her dance card and wrote his name there also. As far as she could see, he was behaving just as a gentleman ought.

"Miss Bavidge."

She turned around, a little embarrassed to have been seen watching Lord Rochester. "Oh, Lord Morton." Her smile became fixed, her cheeks burning. "I... I did not mean..." Wincing inwardly, she took a breath and tried to stop stammering. "It is our dance, then?"

He nodded, although she noticed that he did not smile and appeared to be struggling with some displeasing emotion. His brows were furrowed with one thick line forming between them, his gaze fixed on something just behind her. Not daring to glance behind her for fear of appearing rude, Emma placed a smile on her face and gestured towards the dance floor, hearing the orchestra beginning to play a small introduction that would encourage couples to come forward.

"If you are quite ready, then," she said, making to walk towards the dance floor, only for Lord Morton to reach out and, to her shock, grasp her arm.

"Lord Morton!" she exclaimed, as his hand ran down her arm towards her hand, sending her heart fluttering with both excitement and astonishment. "Whatever are you doing?"

Lord Morton said nothing but let his fingers trail down her hand only to catch her dance card and lift it higher, making Emma lift her hand a little. Blinking rapidly and praying that no one was watching this strange and awkward encounter, Emma could only wait for Lord Morton to finish whatever he was doing, feeling as though she ought to demand an explanation but finding that the words would not come to her.

"Ah." Lord Morton grunted, dropped her dance card and offered his arm. "Shall we go?"

Standing stock still, Emma stared at him, not about to accept his arm without an explanation of what it was he had been doing. "Lord Morton, I—"

"Forgive me." He appeared now a little flustered, his gaze resting anywhere but her face. "I feared that I had approached you for the wrong dance, but it appears I was mistaken." His lips curved, but his smile did not reach his eyes, which, briefly, caught her gaze. "I apologize."

Emma swallowed hard, her skin still prickling from where his fingers had brushed down her arm. It was a reasonable explanation, she supposed, but there had been no reason to touch her in such a manner, especially when they might have been noticed by anyone. The last thing she needed was to have any further rumors spreading through London about her!

Lord Morton cleared his throat as if he were growing impatient. "Might we take to the floor, Miss Bavidge?" he asked, with a tight smile. "The music is about to begin, and we are yet to step out together."

Having found nothing to say and with confusion still whirling about her, Emma accepted his arm and found herself led to the floor by Lord Morton, who walked with quick steps and without a single word coming from his mouth. She took her place, curtsying quickly, as was expected, but found the way that Lord Morton looked at her to be even more unsettling. His expression was still dark, his brows still lowered and his lips taut, as though she had done some sort of wrong to him. Unable to think of what such a thing was, Emma decided to concentrate on the dance, not wanting to make a mistake when she was quite certain that a good many of the *ton* were watching her.

However, as the dance progressed, Emma found herself more and more perplexed by Lord Morton's behavior towards her. There appeared to be no enjoyment in his face as he danced, no happiness in his gaze as he looked at her. It was most unusual, for they had enjoyed an amiable acquaintance thus far, albeit brief. Why then did he appear to be so down in the mouth about their dance? What was the foreboding look in his eyes? And why did he seem so displeased with her?

"Might you tell me, Miss Bavidge, whether or not you have become acquainted with Lord Rochester of late?"

Emma, who was curtsying towards Lord Morton now that the dance had come to a close, looked up at him sharply, seeing a steely glint in his eyes. "Might I ask why you wish to know, Lord Morton?" she asked him, growing a little frustrated with his attitude towards her. "What difference does it make to you who I am acquainted with?"

Lord Morton blinked, as though he had only just realized how strange a question it was. "I..." He trailed off, dropping his head and running one hand over his eyes. "Forgive me, Miss Bavidge. It is only that I seek to protect you."

Rather astonished at this, Emma said nothing but allowed the silence between them to build in the hope that it would encourage him to say more. Watching him closely, she saw how his dark expression began to fade and how his gaze dipped low to the floor. Perhaps he was only now coming to see how improper he had been.

"I do wish that I was able to succeed," he said softly, his words barely reaching her ears such was the quietness of his voice. "But I fear I cannot." He lifted his head and looked straight into her eyes, his expression grave. "Pray, stay away from Lord Rochester, Miss Bavidge."

"Why?" Emma asked, a swirl of anxiety in her stomach. "What is it that he—"

"I can say no more," Lord Morton interrupted, holding up one hand to prevent her flow of questions. "Forgive me, Miss Bavidge. Good evening."

And with that, he bowed, turned, and began to walk away from her, leaving Emma feeling more confused and conflicted than ever.

CHAPTER SEVEN

*N*athaniel lifted his chin as he walked into Lord Marne's residence, trying to settle his tumultuous thoughts and tangled mind. It had been two days since he had last seen Miss Bavidge, and since then, he had been unable to remove her from his thoughts in any way. She had lingered there, his heavy burden still resting on his shoulders as he thought of her.

"Good evening, Lord Morton."

Attempting to smile, Nathaniel greeted his host. "Marne. Good evening. Thank you for the invitation, old chap."

Lord Marne grinned. "Not at all," he replied chuckling. "Now, you must try to smile a little better than you are at present, Morton, else you shall chase all the young ladies away. Do you not want to be considered a suitable match for someone?"

Nathaniel rolled his eyes, knowing full well that his friend was teasing him. "I have not given the matter much consideration," he replied, with an arched brow.

"You know that last year I was caught up with another matter entirely and so this year—"

"This year, you may do as you wish!" Lord Marne replied, clapping Nathaniel on the shoulder and ushering him a little further into the room. "I am well aware of the aid you gave to Lord Knighton—you know that I shall speak nothing of it to anyone, of course—but I do hope that you will be able to find yourself a little less burdened this season." His expression became somewhat serious, reminding Nathaniel of the time he had come to Lord Marne's townhouse last season, when he had been torn by Lord Rochester's broken promises. He had felt the weight of guilt back then also, although Lord Marne, being a decent sort and an excellent friend, had encouraged him not to think of himself as having done anything wrong at all. Lady Marne, a gentle and sweet soul, had been on hand to listen also, giving her opinion on Lord Rochester—which had shown her evident dislike of the fellow, as Nathaniel recalled.

"My dear wife is somewhere amongst the crowd," Lord Marne continued, still urging Nathaniel through the small crowd. "Ah yes, there she is. She is speaking to Lady Smithton, I believe."

Lady Marne, her youthful face alive with interest as she listened to Lady Smithton, suddenly caught sight of her husband and Nathaniel and waved them both over at once. Lord Marne, however, was caught by the arrival of yet another guest and so had to excuse himself, leaving Nathaniel to greet Lady Marne and Lady Smithton alone.

He moved forward quickly, wanting to ensure that he

greeted and thanked the hostess for the invitation also. "Lady Marne, I am very glad to be here this evening," he told her, adding just a hint of exaggeration to his words. "Thank you for inviting me. I know that these soirees of yours can be very enjoyable."

Lady Marne chuckled. "Always so kind, Lord Morton," she said, smiling at him. "Now, are you acquainted with Lady Smithton?"

"I am not," Nathaniel replied, honestly. "Although I will confess to having heard of you, Lady Smithton."

Lady Smithton did not seem to take offense at this, much to Nathaniel's relief. Instead, she smiled and nodded whilst Lady Marne made the introductions, dropping into a quick curtsy which he returned with a bow.

"I can assure you, Lord Morton, that whatever you have heard of me is nothing more than idle gossip," Lady Smithton said once Lady Marne had finished.

"I am not at all inclined to listen to such things regardless," he told her, honestly. "I dislike how society seems to thrive on such things."

Lady Marne nodded firmly. "*That* is something I can vouch for," she replied with a quick smile in Nathaniel's direction. "Lord Morton has an excellent character, Lady Smithton."

"Indeed." Lady Smithton's eyes searched Nathaniel's face curiously, as though she were seeking something but did not yet know where it lay. "I must say, I am glad to hear such accolades, Lord Morton. They are often few and far between, I find!" Nathaniel was about to say more when Lady Smithton beckoned to someone just behind him, and he turned to see none other than Miss Bavidge walking towards them all, her face holding a blank expression. She did not look at him nor greet him but rather waited until Lady Smithton had begun to speak.

"Lord Morton, I believe you are acquainted with Miss Bavidge," Lady Smithton, sounding quite nonchalant, although Nathaniel was suspicious that this meeting had been hastily contrived in Lady Smithton's mind the moment she had heard he was a respectable gentleman. "Now, Miss Bavidge is here with me for this evening, so I did wonder if I might beg a favor from you."

Nathaniel cleared his throat, looking towards Lady Smithton and away from Miss Bavidge, who had a slow red flush creeping up her cheeks. "And what might that be, Lady Smithton?" he asked as calmly as he could, fearing that the lady was going to push himself and Miss Bavidge together when, the truth was, he should be doing what he could to remain apart from her.

"I was hoping that you might sit with Miss Bavidge when the musical performances begin," Lady Smithton said, sounding quite delighted with the prospect. "You see, I have another dear friend that I have quite promised to sit near to when the time comes for the musical part of the evening, and I fear that I would quite neglect Miss Bavidge!" She dimpled at Nathaniel, her eyes glowing with the certainty that came from knowing he could not easily refuse. "What say you?"

Nathaniel knew there was no way out and that he had to answer quickly, not wanting to appear rude. "I would be glad to, Lady Smithton," he said, presenting as much of a joyous demeanor as he could. "Miss Bavidge, if you would be willing, I would be glad to sit with you when the music begins."

Miss Bavidge stammered something and dropped her head.

"Perfect," Lady Smithton said, clapping her hands and startling both Nathaniel and Miss Bavidge, who looked up sharply. "Now, if you might allow me to leave you for a moment, I have just seen Lady Parrington, whom I simply must speak to."

Before Nathaniel could protest, before he could say another word, both Lady Smithton and Lady Marne had gone, leaving him standing beside Miss Bavidge without a single idea of what to say. The last time he had seen her, he had behaved rather poorly and then, upon realizing it, had done nothing to rectify nor even apologize for his past behavior. Instead, he had acted awkwardly and left her without any explanation, which brought a good deal of embarrassment to him when he recalled it. Apparently, Miss Bavidge felt the awkwardness between them also, for her head was a little lowered and her eyes sweeping the floor. There was nothing said by either of them for some minutes, making the tension heighten all the more.

"It seems we are to be thrown together, Miss Bavidge," Nathaniel said, eventually, his voice a little dry. "If you do not wish to, however, you need only say, and I shall be glad to find someone else to stand in my place."

Miss Bavidge looked up sharply. "Even if it is Lord Rochester?"

Nathaniel closed his eyes for a moment, the urge to

tell her everything rushing over him only for him to recall that he could not. "I... I apologize for my previous behavior, Miss Bavidge. It must have appeared most strange to you, and there is very little explanation I can give."

"Other than the fact you believe Lord Rochester is not a gentleman I should draw near to," she finished, still holding him with her gaze. "Although you have not stated why. I would ask that you share such reasons with me now, Lord Morton."

Shaking his head, Nathaniel raked his hand through his hair before he had even realized what he was doing. Dropping his arm, he tried to find something to say, some words to make an explanation, but none came to him.

"You are most exasperating, Lord Morton!" Miss Bavidge exclaimed with a good deal more alacrity than he had thought possible from someone such as she. "You behave in such a curious fashion that I do not think I should ever be able to understand you, not even if I should become well acquainted with you." She sighed heavily and tossed her head, clearly irritated with him, but, much to his surprise, Nathaniel found her suddenly quite captivating. It was a sensation that he had not expected and, as she returned her gaze to him again, Nathaniel felt a stone drop into his stomach, his breath hitching and his mouth going dry.

Miss Bavidge, he had considered, was not a beauty by any standard although he had thought her reasonably pretty. However, now that she held his gaze, Nathaniel felt as if he were seeing her for the first time. The way her blue eyes sparkled with irritation, the way her lips were pressed hard together, her cheeks rather red, as they were accustomed to do whenever she was embarrassed or frustrated, filled him with an awareness of her that swept all through him. A voice in his head told him to say something, to speak to Miss Bavidge about anything he could think of, but his voice simply would not co-operate.

Thankfully, he was saved from further embarrassment by the sound of the musicians beginning to tune their instruments, which caught Miss Bavidge's attention. Turning her head, she looked towards the other side of the room where footmen were just finishing setting out chairs for the guests, ready for them to seat themselves so that they might join the performance.

"Shall we sit down?" Nathaniel managed to say, his throat tight with the emotions that were rushing all through him. "It looks as though the first part of this evening's entertainment is to begin."

Miss Bavidge turned back to him, her eyes filled with a frustration that Nathaniel wished he could remove.

"Yes, I suppose we should," she agreed, her voice a little quieter than before. "But we have some minutes yet with which we might continue our conversation." One eyebrow lifted in silent challenge, but Nathaniel merely shook his head, angered with his own lack of willingness to tell her the truth for fear of what would follow. Was he being selfish by keeping the truth about Lord Rochester to himself? Could he not tell her some of Lord Rochester's character without going into detail so that she would be made aware of the danger that came with being in that gentleman's company?

"Might I surmise, Lord Morton, that for some reason,

you cannot speak of your reasons behind your desire for me to stay away from Lord Rochester?"

Miss Bavidge was speaking quietly now, all sense of irritation gone from her. It was as if she were doing her level best to understand whilst still holding onto her determination to know what it was he was trying to say.

"Indeed, Miss Bavidge," Nathaniel replied, slowly, trying to work out what he could say and what he could not. "I was once friends with Lord Rochester, and I believe that his character has not changed since that time." He recalled how Lord Rochester had, so often, chased after the young ladies that had caught his eye. There had never been the suggestion that Rochester wished to marry any of them, merely that he only wished for them to give him a taste of their affections—going as far as he could push them. Nathaniel had never liked such a characteristic in his friend but, having made his concerns known upon one occasion, had chosen not to say anything more, believing that Rochester knew all too well his thoughts on the matter. Perhaps that had been wrong of him.

"I see," Miss Bavidge replied, calmly, still looking him dead in the eye. "And might I ask why you are so eager to protect me from Lord Rochester, Lord Morton?" Her expression softened just a little as she glanced away for a moment, her color heightening all the more. "After all, even before we were introduced, I was aware of how you watched me, Lord Morton. I was not introduced to Lord Rochester then, so what could be the reason for such an interest?" The tone of her voice grew a little higher as she continued to look away from him, clearly embarrassed to be asking such a thing yet determined to hear the truth from him.

Nathaniel wanted to sink into the ground. He had not expected Miss Bavidge to be so direct, and certainly had not thought she would be asking so many questions of him! Her demands to know the answers send him spiraling back in surprise, his mind searching for responses that he did not have. Miss Bavidge appeared to be almost fierce in her determinations, and he had not seen such a resoluteness before. Had it come from her struggles against the whispers of the *beau monde*? Or was it her new friendship with Lady Smithton that encouraged her so?

"You have not yet answered, Lord Morton, and I find that I am growing agitated waiting for you to do so," Miss Bavidge murmured, taking a small step closer to him. "Why must you be so mysterious?"

Nathaniel caught his breath as another flurry of sensations ran over him. Miss Bavidge was standing nearer to him now, and that small act of taking one small step closer to him had sent his heart bouncing about his chest without any explanation as to why. It was most extraordinary.

"I do not mean to be mysterious," he managed to say, aware of how his voice rasped with suppressed emotion. "I do apologize, Miss Bavidge, but I—"

"My dear friends, if you will come to take your seats, the first musical performance of the evening is about to take place."

Closing his eyes tightly against the wave of exasperation that crashed over him at the sound of Lord Marne's voice, Nathaniel let out his breath slowly before opening his eyes again. Miss Bavidge was not looking irritated, as he had supposed, but rather quite disappointed. Her shoulders slumped, her face turned away as her eyes remained downcast—and Nathaniel felt his heart slam back into place with a sudden, desperate urge.

"Might I call upon you, Miss Bavidge?"

The words had ripped from his mouth before he could prevent them, surprising both himself and Miss Bavidge, who looked at him sharply, her breath catching in an audible gasp.

"Perhaps tomorrow," he stumbled on, not quite certain what he was doing but knowing that, deep in his heart, he did not wish to continue playing this strange game with her. "Or the day after that," he finished, with a tight smile. "Although, if you do not wish to then I—"

"Tomorrow would suit me very well, Lord Morton." Miss Bavidge's expression remained one of astonishment, but she spoke clearly enough. "I thank you. That is a kind offer, and I look forward to speaking with you further. I am engaged to call upon Lady Smithton as my aunt is indisposed tomorrow afternoon, but I know Lady Smithton would be more than glad to have you call on me there." Her smile began to spread across her face, her eyes lowering demurely. "We should sit down," she said, walking away from him with short, hasty steps.

Nathaniel followed after her numbly, not quite certain what he had done. The awareness that he had asked to call upon Miss Bavidge began to roll about his mind, sending a prickle of uneasiness up his spine. What was it he intended to do by calling on her? Had it merely been a reaction to her pressing questions, a way to escape having to answer her? Or was it that, deep within his heart, there was something more to what he felt and thought of Miss Bavidge? Yes, he had been watching her since her return to London, and yes, he did feel some protectiveness over her as well as guilt over the part he had played in her difficulties, but to have any sort of attraction towards the lady was not something he had ever expected.

But still, despite knowing that he ought to remove himself from Miss Bavidge's side as best he could, Nathaniel found himself feeling a little pleased that Miss Bavidge had accepted his request. He had no thought as to what he would say to her tomorrow for, of course, the questions were certain to return, but he would allow himself to worry about such a thing when the time came. For the present, he was simply going to enjoy the rest of the evening as he continued to sit with Miss Bavidge. He would allow every emotion, every hint of feeling, to wash over him and thereafter linger in his heart, should it wish to do so. Once he was alone, once he had time to think, then he might reflect on what it was that his heart was beginning to feel for the determined and astute Miss Bavidge.

CHAPTER EIGHT

"And you say he is to call upon you later this afternoon?"

Emma smiled and nodded, all too aware of how her cheeks were beginning to warm at the mention of Lord Morton. The flaring of her cheeks was often something that occurred, she knew, for it happened whenever she was angry, frustrated, or a little embarrassed. It also seemed to occur whenever she caught sight of or even mentioned Lord Morton, which was most peculiar.

"I think Lord Morton might turn out to be a very suitable gentleman," Miss Crosby continued, throwing Emma a quick smile. "Does Lady Smithton approve of him?"

"She does," Emma replied quickly, although a slight stab of guilt entered her heart as she recalled how she had not spoken to Lady Smithton of her confusing conversations with Lord Morton as regarding Lord Rochester. She would have to do so, for she had promised to be honest with Lady Smithton so that the lady, in turn, could guide and help her. However, if Lord Morton continued to be as attentive as he had been last evening, aside from the strange conversation about Lord Rochester, then mayhap Emma would not have need of her assistance for much longer. The thought brought a flurry of excitement to Emma's heart and she resisted the urge to fan her face with her hand, aware of just how rosy her cheeks must be.

"And what of you?" she asked her friend, seeing Miss Crosby look away. "Have you made any progress?"

Miss Crosby sighed heavily but kept her gaze away from Emma's. "There is a slight... difficulty in my present circumstance," she replied carefully. "I have told all to Lady Smithton, of course, and she is doing her level best to advise me." She laughed softly, her eyes twinkling as the tension that had been in her frame only seconds ago began to fade. "And Lord Havisham has done a remarkable job of ensuring I am introduced to as many people as possible."

Emma laughed at this. "Lord Havisham attended a ball for your sake and then a musical soiree for mine," she chuckled, recalling just how Lord Havisham had done his best for her also. "I am certain he shall be quite worn out very soon! Is he not to go to the theatre this evening with Lady Smithton and Lady Amelia?"

"Indeed," Miss Crosby replied, aware of how Lord Havisham had stifled a groan when Lady Smithton asked it of him. Lord Havisham had spoken of his lack of interest in the theatre on occasion before, including how he found the plays dull and the atmosphere stifling. He would not choose to go to it—but, again, he was willing to do so regardless.

"I do not think he does it for our sake only, however," Miss Crosby continued, observantly. "Lady Smithton is, I think, rather dear to him."

Nodding, Emma let her smile soften, wondering if she would ever have a gentleman considering her in the same way. "That is more than apparent, yes," she agreed, quietly. "I do wonder why Lady Smithton does not accept his court."

Miss Crosby let out a soft chuckle. "I do believe that if you are an independent, wealthy young widow, then you have the freedom to do just as you please whenever you please," she replied with a wry smile. "If I found myself in such a position, then I might enjoy my independence for a time also, even if someone such as Lord Havisham sought to court me!"

Emma considered this for a few moments and was about to add her thoughts to their discussion, only to hear someone call her name. Much to her surprise, she turned her head and came to a stop, only to see none other than Lord Rochester approaching them, a broad smile on his face.

"Did that gentleman just call to you from across the park?" Miss Crosby asked, speaking to her out of the corner of her mouth. "That is a little rude, is it not?"

Biting her lip, Emma had no time to answer, for Lord Rochester had a long stride and was soon too close to them for her to reply to Miss Crosby. She did think that Lord Rochester was a *little* rude in the way he had called out to her but, then again, how else was he to garner her attention? Thankful that the park was not overly busy with patrons, Emma curtsied quickly as Lord Rochester inclined his head, her mind filled with warnings about Lord Rochester's intentions.

"Good afternoon, Miss Bavidge!" Lord Rochester exclaimed, loudly. "How wonderful that we should happen to meet on such a fine day as this!" His gaze drifted quickly towards Miss Crosby, and Emma quickly stammered an introduction, still not quite certain what it was that he intended by approaching her in such a fashion.

"I am glad to make your acquaintance, Miss Crosby," Lord Rochester said, with a broad smile that gave him the appearance of amiability. "I do hope you are enjoying the season thus far."

Miss Crosby said that yes, she was, and then suggested that the three of them walk for a time together so that they were not blocking the path for others and, much to Emma's surprise, Lord Rochester agreed at once, obviously eager to spend a little more time with them.

If only I knew the reasons as to why Lord Morton fears for me should I continue this acquaintance, she thought to herself, as Lord Rochester and Miss Crosby fell into easy conversation. Yes, Lord Morton had spoken of his concern over Lord Rochester's character, but that did not give her any particular insight into what it was specifically that Lord Morton disliked. As far as she could see, Lord Rochester was a decent gentleman who did not shy away from her nor spread gossip about her once they had enjoyed a dance or a small conversation. She had not seen him rushing to his acquaintances to laugh and point in her direction, which surely spoke well of his character. Unless it was all a façade and she the unwitting fool.

"You are quiet this afternoon, Miss Bavidge."

Jerking slightly in surprise, having been tugged from her thoughts so swiftly, Emma looked up to see Lord Rochester looking down at her with a small smile on his face, his eyes twinkling. Despite herself, she blushed furiously and turned her head a little away from him, praying that he would not notice.

"I... I was lost in thought, Lord Rochester," she replied, honestly. "Forgive me."

Lord Rochester chuckled. "Not at all, Miss Bavidge," he replied, as Miss Crosby came to fall into step beside her so that they walked three abreast along the wide path. "I find it quite pleasing that a young lady should be so caught up with her own thoughts that she has to be pulled from them. I consider it a mark of intelligence." He gave her another broad smile, clearly trying to put her at ease. "Might I ask what you were thinking of?"

Emma blinked rapidly, trying to find something to say which would answer his question but without revealing the truth. Her tongue stuck to the roof of her mouth, the palms of her hands growing hot and sweaty as she tried to find an answer.

"But, then again, you will think me most rude to be asking such pressing questions," Lord Rochester continued with a chuckle. "I do apologize, Miss Bavidge. You must be permitted to keep your thoughts to yourself without feeling any urgency to share them with the likes of me."

"I thank you," Emma replied, weakly, not quite

managing to force her lips into a smile. "You are most understanding, Lord Rochester."

He smiled at her again, his expression amiable enough, but still Emma could not let go of the warnings that continued to hurtle through her mind. For whatever reason, she found herself trusting Lord Morton more than she would Lord Rochester, which meant that she gave his words a good deal more weight than any Lord Rochester might speak.

"Have you been enjoying the season thus far, Lord Rochester?" she asked, not quite certain whether or not such a question had already been asked or answered given that she had not been listening to Lord Rochester and Miss Crosby's conversation. "I do hope that you—"

"It has been quite wonderful!" Lord Rochester exclaimed, interrupting her. "I have enjoyed every soiree, every ball, every play that I have attended. Which reminds me, Miss Bavidge..." Trailing off, he moved a little closer to her as they walked, his eyes resting on hers and holding them fiercely. "Might you consider attending the theatre with me?"

Emma's stomach turned over, her heart quickening in her chest as she looked up into Lord Rochester's face. She did not know what to say, for the urge to remain as far away from Lord Rochester as she could grew steadily within her, remembering the fierce look on Lord Morton's face as he had spoken of the gentleman.

"There is a delightful little play that I think you would greatly enjoy," Lord Rochester continued, no anxiety in his voice or concern in his eyes as he lifted his gaze from hers and settled it back on the path ahead. "It would be a most enjoyable evening, Miss Bavidge, I am quite certain of it."

Swallowing what appeared to be a large amount of dust in her mouth and attempting to speak as clearly as she could, Emma let out a long breath and tried to find a way to express herself in such a manner that would not offend Lord Rochester. Even though she did not know the truth of his character nor the reasons behind Lord Morton's urging to keep away from the fellow, Emma found herself disinclined to further her acquaintance with him. This was made all the more apparent when she considered just how her heart had leaped in her chest when Lord Morton had asked to call upon her and how it fluttered whenever she thought of it.

"My goodness, Miss Bavidge, you are to be quite spoiled it seems!" Miss Crosby laughed, linking arms with Emma and shaking her head in evident surprise. "Now you have not only one gentleman seeking to spend more time with you, but two, in fact!" She smiled brightly at Lord Rochester, clearly delighted for Emma—but Emma felt herself slowly sinking into the ground, embarrassed and mortified that her friend had spoken so foolishly.

Lord Rochester's expression changed almost at once. Instead of smiling back at Miss Crosby and making some remark about how it was understandable that Miss Bavidge should have more than one gentleman eager to spend time in her company, he began to frown, his lips thinning and his brows lowering over his eyes. The change was quite remarkable, for he no longer appeared handsome, but rather almost malevolent in his expression. Emma's toes curled in her shoes as she came to a stop, trying to laugh at Miss Crosby's remark but finding that the sound stuck in her throat.

"I am lucky indeed, yes," she agreed, seeing how Miss Crosby flushed darkly as she realized what she had said and how outspoken she had been. "But I am sorry I cannot accept as I have a previous engagement, Lord Rochester. I do thank you for your invitation." She placed a smile on her lips, only for Lord Rochester to frown all the more, his eyes searching her face as though she had a secret he wanted to discover. Emma's very soul seemed to shake, sending a tremor through her as she looked back at him, doing her best not to flinch.

"Another gentleman is seeking to court you, Miss Bavidge?" Lord Rochester asked, his voice a good deal lower than before. "That is... interesting."

Emma lifted her chin and tried not to allow his appearance to intimidate her. "I am flattered at the attention, of course," she told him, keeping her voice calm. "And I am very grateful for it."

Lord Rochester said nothing for some moments, his jaw working hard as he looked back at her, unblinking and intense in his gaze.

"I must inform you that I am quite serious in my intentions, Miss Bavidge," Lord Rochester murmured, a gleam in his eye that Emma found she did not like. "I should like to court you, if you would agree to it."

Emma's answer came to her lips immediately. "That is most kind of you, Lord Rochester," she replied, seeing Miss Crosby drop her head with embarrassment at being present for such a private moment. "But as yet, I have not decided upon accepting anyone's court. I may be enjoying the company of others, but that does not mean that my mind had settled upon one individual." She hoped that this might make Lord Rochester think that she was being called upon by not only one but perhaps two or three other gentlemen, praying that this would prevent Lord Rochester from asking any more questions, but all it seemed to do was make Lord Rochester's expression darken a little more.

"Then I must hope that you will allow me to prove myself to you," he replied with a jerk of his head, which Emma thought was meant to be the smallest of bows. "Might I know the name of the other gentleman who appears so eager to pursue you, Miss Bavidge?" His eyes lit with interest, his lip curling slightly. "It is best to know one's enemy, I believe."

Emma tried to laugh, waving a hand in his direction. "Lord Rochester, you are quite ridiculous. Surely you cannot expect me to give you the name of this gentleman simply because you wish to *defeat* him in some way!" She shook her head, forcing a teasing smile to her lips. "After all, it is I who shall decide my future, is it not? Therefore, your awareness of such things matters very little."

Lord Rochester leaned forward, looking her dead in the eye and narrowing his gaze slightly. Emma trembled visibly although, with an effort, she put a smile on her face and held his gaze.

"It is Lord Morton, is it not?" he asked, his voice barely louder than a whisper as he arched one thick eyebrow. "He is the other gentleman you speak of."

Emma felt as though she had been pushed into a tub

of cold water, for it seemed to run down her back in rivulets, sending another tremor all through her. She could not find anything to say, and it was her silence that seemed to confirm to Lord Rochester that what he had guessed was correct.

Lord Rochester sighed heavily, shook his head and ran one hand over his eyes. "Pray, Miss Bavidge, do not become another young lady caught by the outwardly kind appearance that Lord Morton presents to the *beau monde*," he said, sending another wave of cold water over her. "You must know that he is not a gentleman of good character."

Emma hesitated, seeing Miss Crosby look up, startled. "I am not quite certain that such a statement is true, Lord Rochester," she told him slowly, knowing that Lady Smithton would not have encouraged her to accept Lord Morton if she believed him to be a gentleman of poor character. "But I thank you for your consideration."

"Oh, but it is quite true!" Lord Rochester exclaimed, fervently. "I must speak to you of this, Miss Bavidge, if only to warn you."

Wanting to close her eyes and sigh heavily, Emma restrained herself with an effort and, instead, simply held Lord Rochester's gaze and allowed him to speak. There seemed to be no good in attempting to silence him, for he was quite eager to speak, and she did not think he would be restrained. The dark expression had left his face now, his eyes shining with an enthusiasm that could not be dampened.

"Lord Morton and I were once very close companions," he told her, echoing what Lord Morton himself had said. "However, it was due to his conduct that our friendship is no more, and, for that, I must make certain to warn you from his side."

Emma tilted her head carefully, feeling the cold drain from her, leaving her a little more in control of the conversation. "His conduct?" she repeated, wondering why she had heard the same from Lord Morton about Lord Rochester as she was now hearing from Lord Rochester himself. "What about his conduct set you both asunder?" Seeing Lord Rochester hesitate and look away, she frowned heavily, her eyes sharp. "Surely you cannot imagine that I would be willing to simply accept your word about his character without some sort of explanation, Lord Rochester!"

At this, Lord Rochester sighed heavily and dropped his head, his hands rubbing at the lines on his forehead. "I suppose I cannot ask you to do such a thing, no," he murmured as Emma shot a quick look towards Miss Crosby, who was still standing to her left, shifting uncomfortably on her feet.

"Then might I suggest that you speak honestly to me, Lord Rochester, for else I shall not know what to think," she told him, firmly, although she did not tell the gentleman that Lord Morton had given her much the same warning as was now running from Lord Rochester's mouth. "Pray, do tell me what you can."

Lord Rochester nodded slowly, lifting his head and looking straight at her. "I shall do precisely that, Miss Bavidge," he agreed, quickly. "But now it is not convenient to do so." A quick look towards Miss Crosby had

Emma's eyes narrowing just a little, wondering if the man was using Miss Crosby's presence as an excuse.

"Then when would be?" she asked, her expression tight. "As I have said, I have a requirement for you to speak honestly with me."

"I am well aware of that," Lord Rochester replied quickly. "Shall we say Thursday evening, if you are not already engaged?"

Emma blinked, a little confused. "Thursday evening?"

"Capital!" Lord Rochester boomed, suddenly overwhelming her with his presence as a broad grin settled on his face. "I shall send details, of course, but I am already looking forward to accompanying you to the theatre, Miss Bavidge. We shall be able to speak privately then." He swept into a bow as Emma began to stammer, her cheeks flaring with heat as she realized what Lord Rochester intended. She had not agreed to attend the theatre with him, but he was, it seemed, quite determined that this should be the case.

"*Do* give my regards to Lord Morton," Lord Rochester finished, with a smile that appeared more ugly than genuine. "And I shall see you on Thursday, Miss Bavidge. Good afternoon."

He bowed again, gave her another smile, and then turned on his heel and walked quickly away from them both, leaving Emma stammering and spluttering after him. A long silence followed as Miss Crosby simply stood there, her hands clasped in front of her and her head bowed low.

"Goodness," Emma murmured eventually, trying to

make sense of what had just occurred, as well as her concerning feelings over what Lord Rochester had said about Lord Morton. "It seems I am to go to the theatre with Lord Rochester, then." This had her frowning, for she did not like the feeling that she had been persuaded to do something without having had any intention of doing so in the first place. Lord Rochester appeared to be a little conniving, and this brought her a good deal of unease.

"I am sorry, Emma," Miss Crosby said, her head still low and her voice barely loud enough to hear. "I did not mean to do such a foolish thing. It was quite unintentional and I—"

"You need not concern yourself, Sarah," Emma interrupted, smiling at her friend despite the whirling sense of unease that was settling in her stomach. "Please, do not feel guilty over such a thing. It was an innocent mistake, and I am, in a way, grateful for it."

"Oh?" Miss Crosby's head lifted, and she looked back at Emma in surprise.

Emma began to walk along the path again, her friend falling into step beside her. "Whilst I will not pretend I am not very confused over what each gentleman has said about the other, at least I am fully aware of their concerns about the other."

"But how shall you know the truth?" Sarah asked as they turned around to make their way out of the park. "How shall you discover which concerns are genuine and which have no basis in truth?"

Hesitating, Emma allowed a vision of Lord Morton to swim in front of her eyes, feeling the urgent desire to believe him over Lord Rochester run through her. "It is something of a mystery, yes," she agreed, quietly. "But all mysteries need to be solved, do they not?" Her resolve grew steadily, her mind filled with both Lord Rochester and Lord Morton's words. "Somewhere, in the midst of it all, lies the truth, and I am quite determined to discover it, no matter what it may cost me."

athaniel had not expected to feel such a whirlwind of emotion flood him as he stepped into the drawing room to see both Miss Bavidge and Lady Smithton rising to greet him. His thoughts had been filled with all sorts of questions and concerns over what it was that would be awaiting him, and now, as he bowed before them both, he found his mind quickening all the more.

"Good afternoon, Lady Smithton, Miss Bavidge." He tried to smile, aware of just how furiously his heart was beating. Why was he in such a turmoil over Miss Bavidge when, previously, he had felt nothing but concern over her presence within society? Something had changed within him drastically, something that burned through his heart and mind and forced him to reconsider everything he thought he had decided.

"Good afternoon, Lord Morton," Lady Smithton replied as Miss Bavidge gave him a small smile which,

Nathaniel noticed, did not quite reach her eyes. "Please, do be seated."

"I thank you." Hurrying to the indicated chair, he sat down at once, feeling a strange sense of tension fill the room as he looked from Lady Smithton to Miss Bavidge and back again. Was it because Miss Bavidge felt as uncomfortable as he did? Or was there something more that he was, as yet, not entirely aware of?

"Miss Bavidge," he began, stammering just a little and betraying his nervousness as he did so. "I... I do hope that you have had a pleasant day thus far." It was a foolish thing to say and certainly a little ridiculous, but such was the gnawing nervousness within him that he had no consideration of what else there was for him to say or discuss with her.

"I did," Miss Bavidge replied as Lady Smithton rose from her chair, her skirts rustling. She moved to the window at the other end of the room, making it quite clear that Miss Bavidge and Nathaniel were to have some time to talk without her presence. Nathaniel, whilst grateful, felt his tongue sticking to the roof of his mouth, not at all certain what he should say next.

"In fact," Miss Bavidge continued, a little tightly, "I met with an acquaintance in the park as I was out walking with Miss Crosby."

"Oh?" Nathaniel gave her a small smile, feeling his tension begin to fade as he saw how she was trying to discuss matters with him. "Did you have an enjoyable walk? The afternoon has been very fine."

Miss Bavidge said nothing for a moment, biting her lip and looking at him with an unblinking gaze.

"I did," she murmured, after a few moments. "I had an excellent walk with Miss Crosby, Lord Morton. I was surprised, however, when Lord Rochester appeared and began to fall into step with us both."

Nathaniel blinked rapidly, his heart dropping to the floor only to bounce up and slam hard into his chest again.

"As you can imagine, I was a trifle reluctant to walk and speak with the gentleman, after what you had said to me about him," Miss Bavidge continued with a wave of her hand. "But thereafter, he also became aware of your intention to call upon me this afternoon."

Frowning, Nathaniel began to nod slowly. "I see," he replied, carefully, not quite certain what Miss Bavidge meant by such a thing and feeling an uncomfortable tension begin to settle within his heart all over again. "And I am certain that Lord Rochester had his own thoughts on that." He tried to give her a wry smile, only for it to scrape at his lips in a half-hearted attempt before fading away completely.

"Yes, he did," Miss Bavidge replied, her light blue eyes fixed upon his as a spot of color began to burn in each cheek. "Much to my surprise, Lord Morton, he gave me much the same warning as you have done about him."

His mouth went dry as he looked into Miss Bavidge's face and saw her looking back at him with a questioning expression. What was it she wanted to know? Did she expect him to confirm that whatever Lord Rochester had said about him was true? What was it precisely that Lord Rochester had said? His heart sank like a heavy weight, wondering if Lord Rochester had told Miss Bavidge exactly what Nathaniel had done when it came to her father.

"You have nothing to say on this, Lord Morton?" Miss Bavidge asked, her voice a little softer. "You have no response?"

"How can I," he asked, honestly, "when I do not know what it is that has been said of me?"

Miss Bavidge let out a long, heavy sigh and shook her head. "I confess that I do not know what to think, Lord Morton," she told him as the door behind them opened to reveal a maid carrying in a few trays of refreshments, although nothing whetted Nathaniel's appetite, such was his nervousness. "There is something more within this situation, I am quite certain of it, but I am also certain that neither of you will be willing to speak of it to me with any degree of honesty."

"That is not fair to say," Nathaniel retorted, his words a little brash without his intending them to be so. He saw Miss Bavidge recoil a little and closed his eyes tightly, trying to reign in his flare of temper. "I would speak to you of the truth, Miss Bavidge, if I did not fear that it would bring even more of a struggle to you."

Miss Bavidge nodded slowly, her gaze still fixed and intense. "I see," she said, slowly, although she did not appear to be convinced by anything he said. "Then I shall have to hear the truth from Lord Rochester, it seems, for he has promised to speak to me of it in its entirety when we go to the theatre later on this week." She arched a brow at him in a silent challenge, but Nathaniel felt his heart shrink back in dismay, his courage beginning to fail him.

"I must confess that I did not expect you to go near to Lord Rochester again," he said, his voice tense as a small flicker of anger burnt up his spine. "I thought I had given you adequate warning, Miss Bavidge."

This, however, did not have the effect that Nathaniel had hoped, for instead of nodding and accepting that he had done what he could to protect her, Miss Bavidge suddenly stiffened, her shoulders lifting about her ears in clear tension.

"I do not think, Lord Morton, that you have any right to tell me what I can or cannot do," she replied, tersely. "You may advise me, of course, but since I do not know the intricacies of why you distrust Lord Rochester, you cannot simply expect me to accept it without question." She spread her hands, letting out a slow breath as though to calm her frustrations. "As I have said, you are being somewhat mysterious, and I find that the more I consider it, the more confused and frustrated I become."

"That has not been my intention," Nathaniel responded, immediately. "I am doing what I can to keep you from danger, Miss Bavidge—"

"Without giving me any explanation as to why that might be, Lord Morton," she said directly, looking at him straight in the eye. "Nor have you explained why you sought me out from the very first moment I arrived in London, although we did not formally meet until some-time later." The echoes of their conversation the previous night drifted back to him, making him aware that Miss Bavidge was determined to discover the truth, no matter what it would take. "Might I give you this opportunity to explain yourself, Lord Morton?"

So saying, Miss Bavidge placed her hands together tightly in her lap and looked at him, her head tilting a little to the left as she studied him. Her questions remained hanging in the air between them, leaving his breathing ragged as he felt the room closing in about him. There was nowhere to hide. He would have to speak the truth, and yet the fear of what it would do began to bite at his heart.

Swallowing hard, he licked his lips and tried to put his thoughts into coherent order. Knowing that Lady Smithton was also present, he let out his breath slowly and closed his eyes.

"The reason I sought you out, Miss Bavidge," he said softly, not able to look at her, "was because I feared for what your reception might be. I was... aware of what had gone on with your father and therefore..." Shaking his head, Nathaniel hesitated for a moment, not quite certain of what her response would be. "Therefore, I wanted to ensure that I could aid your passage somewhat in any way I could." This, he realized, was a very poor explanation and certainly did not go into detail about his part in her father's fall from grace, but it was the most he could manage at the present.

"Might I ask, Lord Morton, why you had such consideration for Miss Bavidge?" Lady Smithton asked, suddenly reappearing beside Miss Bavidge, her eyes flickering with interest. "Why is it that she, out of all the young ladies touched by scandal, was the only one you considered?"

Nathaniel felt a flush creep up his throat but held Lady Smithton's gaze steadily, his heart thumping furiously. "She was the only one I was aware of," he replied, honestly. "I knew none other that had been 'touched by scandal,' as you say. I am not one inclined to listen to gossip and, therefore, I had no similar concerns for any other young ladies who were in similar straits." This, at least, was the truth, and that meant he could speak without hesitation, for no uneasiness nor guilt bit at his heart. Instead, he looked from one to the other, seeing how Miss Bavidge's expression had softened, how her eyes seemed almost alight as she glanced up at Lady Smithton.

"I see," Lady Smithton replied, giving him a small smile, before looking back at Miss Bavidge. "Does this satisfy you, Miss Bavidge?"

Nathaniel held his breath, the truth still burning in his mind but searing his mouth so hot that he could not speak another word.

"In a way," Miss Bavidge answered, slowly, her gaze still lingering on his face. "I am touched, I suppose, by your concern for me, although I must wonder why Lord Rochester speaks so ill of you." Her lips thinned for a moment. "He means to speak to me on Thursday evening of your poor character, Lord Morton. This goes entirely against what you have said about yourself, for a gentleman who considers others and is aware of the unfortunate consequences that falls upon shoulders such as mine does not, I think, make a gentleman's character rather questionable."

Seeing a sudden opportunity, Nathaniel leaped for it at once. "You have known that Lord Rochester and I were once friends, as I have said to you on a previous occasion," he began, seeing her nod. "Did Lord Rochester also confirm such a thing?"

"He did," Miss Bavidge agreed, quickly.

"Then there must have been a reason for our friendship to come to an end, must there not?" he queried, seeing both Miss Bavidge and Lady Smithton watching him closely. "I should tell you, Miss Bavidge, that the reason our friendship came to an end was simply because I realized I could not trust him."

Miss Bavidge blinked but said nothing, her lips twisting just a little. Lady Smithton interjected, her own curiosity apparent. "Did he fail you in some way?"

"He did," Nathaniel stated, wondering just how much of the truth he could give away without endangering himself. "I spoke to him about a matter that was both private and important. However, he did not keep it to himself, as I had hoped." Swallowing hard as the same emotions of anger and betrayal began to haunt him, Nathaniel looked back Miss Bavidge and prayed silently that she would not ask him about the specifics of the matter. "Therefore, I knew that I could no longer trust him. His behavior towards the young ladies of the *ton* had concerned me, and whilst I had spoken to him of my worries previously, I considered the matter was between himself and his conscience. I did not expect that there should be anything that would injure me personally, but on that regard, I was proven wrong." He lifted one shoulder in a half shrug, not revealing the depths of his pain. "The truth is, Miss Bavidge, as petty as it may seem, Lord Rochester holds me in contempt for my steadfast desire to bring our friendship to a close. He thinks me judgmental, and mayhap, in that regard, I am, but I consider trust to be of the most vital importance between friends. Therefore, I could not in good conscience continue."

Thus said, Nathaniel sat back in his chair, aware that there was nothing else he wished to say at the present. He had told Miss Bavidge as much of the truth as he could and, whilst he had not mentioned how he involved himself in the matter between her father and the Earl of Knighton, Nathaniel considered that he had dealt rather well with the difficulties that faced him. Yes, he had not been entirely truthful, but Miss Bavidge did not need to know that particular fact as yet.

Although she will need to become aware of it at some time, if you are set on courting her.

The thought startled him, sending a rush of heat all through him as he let the words linger in his mind. He had told himself that calling upon Miss Bavidge had been a mere distraction so as to end their conversation the previous night, but now that he reflected upon it, the idea of courting her did not seem at all unpleasant. In fact, he found his desire to do so growing quite steadily, increasing with almost every second that passed. His heart trembled within him, making him fear what he might say next should Miss Bavidge be willing to accept what he had said thus far.

"You mean no ill will towards Miss Bavidge I think," Lady Smithton murmured, her gaze intense but gentle. "Your concern, from what I have seen, is genuine and that should be merited to you."

Nathaniel nodded fervently, accepting what Lady

Smithton had said but speaking directly to Miss Bavidge herself. "I assure you, Miss Bavidge, as Lady Smithton has astutely stated, I have no ill will toward you. My intentions are clear. I have nothing within my character that should cause you any concern; I give you my word."

At this, Lady Smithton leaned over and murmured something in Miss Bavidge's ear, something that Nathaniel could not make out. His heart was racing, his mind working through all the different outcomes that could follow this conversation. If he had done well, then mayhap Miss Bavidge would be willing to forgo her conversation with Lord Rochester, which meant he could work out a way to speak to her about her father's situation —but in his own time and without any threat from Lord Rochester.

However, she might very well accept his explanations but still wish to speak to Lord Rochester himself, which would mean that he had no hope of courting her further. He would be gone from her presence, thrown from her side. Nothing he would do thereafter would mean anything to her.

"I am grateful for your willing explanation," Miss Bavidge said slowly, her brows knotted as she considered him. "It would be rude of me to pry further into the matters that you speak of, for they were clearly between yourself and Lord Rochester." She hesitated, her lip caught between her teeth for a moment as she studied him. "Lady Smithton has set store by you, Lord Morton, and I believe that my heart is inclined to do so also. Therefore," she finished, with a slightly embarrassed smile, "I should be glad of your visits and your company at any time, Lord Morton. And I shall take your advice as it regards Lord Rochester."

A weight rolled off Nathaniel's shoulders as he inclined his head, feeling the pressure that had been building within him suddenly fading away. "I am grateful for that, Miss Bavidge," he said, his relief pouring out of him. "For I should like to call upon you a little more frequently, I think."

Lady Smithton let out a laugh that made Nathaniel flush with mortification.

"You only 'think' you wish to see Miss Bavidge again, Lord Morton?" she asked, teasingly. "You do not know for certain?"

Nathaniel stammered a response, trying to state that yes, he did wish to see Miss Bavidge again and that he was certain of it, only to see Lady Smithton smiling broadly and a gleam of mischief in Miss Bavidge's eyes.

He was making a cake of himself.

"If you would permit it, Lady Smithton," he said, trying to form his words so that they were clear and decisive. "I should like to seek to court Miss Bavidge, if I may." The intention in his mind began to grow steadily, his heart beating with the firm confirmation that yes, this was precisely what he wanted. "That is, Miss Bavidge, I should like to court you if you would be willing to accept me." The air between them grew thick as Nathaniel looked across the room into Miss Bavidge's eyes, seeing the flicker of uncertainty there. His courage quelled for a moment, fearing that she would refuse him, only for Miss Bavidge to sigh and nod, her cheeks turning a gentle shade of red as she looked away.

Nathaniel thought her beautiful.

"A walk, mayhap?" he asked, his happiness mounting each second. "Or the theatre?"

Miss Bavidge laughed softly, although Nathaniel did not know why.

"The theatre would be quite spectacular," she replied, with a quick smile. "Shall we say, Thursday evening?"

A flush crashed over Nathaniel as he realized what she meant by that. She would choose him over any other gentleman; would choose to spend time with him instead of spending time with Lord Rochester. This brought with it wonderful thoughts, happiness and regret dancing together, intertwined and filling him completely.

"I would be glad to accompany you to the theatre on Thursday evening," he told her without missing a beat. "More than contented, Miss Bavidge. I thank you." He rose to take his leave, seeing how both Miss Bavidge and Lady Smithton were smiling at him. "Good afternoon to you both." Bowing smartly, he moved quickly towards the door and walked straight through it, feeling as though he were walking on the clouds in the sky.

CHAPTER TEN

The truth was, Emma reflected, that being in the company of Lord Morton was one of the most delightful times of her day. He had been most attentive towards her these last few days and, much to her surprise, she had begun to find herself looking forward to his daily visits. Sometimes they would walk, sometimes they would stay within the house and speak about so many things—but no matter what they did, Emma had found herself enjoying every moment.

Emma felt a deep but gentle fondness in her heart for Lord Morton. It was not something she had ever expected, and certainly more than she had ever anticipated! Lady Smithton had been the most helpful of guides, giving her encouragement when she had needed it and allowing her to talk about all that she felt whenever the need was there. Given that Emma's aunt was still quite unwilling to engage with her at almost any social occasion, Emma was hugely grateful to Lady Smithton and her willingness to come alongside her so that she would not be alone. Lady Smithton had been her chaperone, her confidante, and now, her friend. Lord Havisham too, had done his part, for he had sought to discover the truth of Lord Morton's character and had been able to do so rather quickly. Much to Emma's relief, it appeared that Lord Morton was precisely the sort of gentleman he had promised her he considered himself to be: thoughtful, compassionate, and less than eager to throw himself into any of society's vices—including the rumor mills.

Walking slowly through the small bookshop, Emma let her mind go back to the previous night when she had walked with Lord Morton into the theatre. Lady Smithton had accompanied them, of course, but there had still been a good many exclamations over her presence beside Lord Morton. She, who was so stained by her father's sins, was now walking beside a respected gentleman who clearly had taken an interest in her. It was more than many had expected, of course, but Emma did not care. She did not listen to a single whisper, choosing simply to hold her head high and enjoy the performance. It had been excellent, and she had thoroughly enjoyed the evening. Lord Morton had proven to be a wonderful companion, for he had spoken at length to her with both wit and intelligence during the interval and then again afterwards. She had not expected him to make any forward gestures and, thus far, he had not done so, and for that, she was grateful. He was behaving like the perfect gentlemen, which she was beginning to believe him to be.

The only dark spot of the evening had been the presence of Lord Rochester, who had attended the theatre with another young lady instead of with Emma, as had been previously arranged. Emma had not felt any regret in turning Lord Rochester down, nor for sending him a note that made it quite plain that she did not want his continued attentions any longer. She had written that she had made a very simple mistake in having accepted his offer to attend the theatre; she had forgotten that she had already engaged herself that evening to another. Having mentioned this, she also continued on to state that she was now courting another gentlemen and, therefore, did not require his attentions any longer.

It had been brief but direct, which she hoped meant that Lord Rochester would have no more great concerns and would not feel the urge to come to her side and begin to spout more unfavorable comments regarding Lord Morton—comments which Emma was not particularly inclined to believe. The gentleman who was so willing to disparage another was not a gentleman she wished to acquaint herself with, no matter how handsome or genteel he was.

Lord Rochester had walked past both herself and Lord Morton during their time at the theatre, although Emma had been able to tell that Lord Rochester had not recognized them for a moment or two. They had almost walked past him and his companion before Lord Rochester said a single word. The name of Lord Morton had practically exploded from his lips as he had come to see them, his mouth hanging a little ajar as he turned to glare at them both.

Emma had disliked him all the more and had not given him more than a few curt words before continuing on their way, not paying him any particular attention. She was quite determined in her mind that Lord Rochester was not the sort of gentleman one could trust, for he had not responded to her note nor even greeted her as they passed in the theatre. He had simply shouted Lord Morton's name and appeared utterly furious for one reason or the other.

"I must speak to you, Miss Bavidge!" Lord Rochester had called, making her face turn scarlet with embarrassment as she had walked away. "It is of the utmost importance!"

Closing her eyes, Emma let out a long breath and tried to steady herself. There was no need to think of Lord Rochester any longer. Lord Morton had been wise to advise her to stay far from him, and in listening to him and doing as he advised, she had found that every word he had spoken about Lord Rochester had been true. Lord Morton had, as far as she was concerned, proven himself, and that meant a great deal.

Hearing a quiet murmur of voices in one corner of the bookshop, Emma turned her head to see where the sound was coming from—only to gasp in shock. A gentleman and a lady were ensconced together, with the gentleman standing much too close to the lady to be in any way proper. Emma did not know what to do, for the scene made her hot with embarrassment. Turning her head away, she made to look for Miss Crosby and Lady Smithton, who were in the bookshop with her, only to hear the unmistakable sound of Lord Rochester's voice.

Emma froze, hearing him chuckle darkly, as the young lady with him murmured something that was light and breathless with apparent anticipation. Emma closed her eyes and swallowed hard, fearing that the young lady was being dragged into a situation that could have dire consequences for her if she were not careful. Most likely, Lord Rochester had promised the girl that he was true in his affections, that he cared for her in some way so that her defenses would be lowered and he could take from her what he pleased.

She took in a long breath, feeling the urge to do *something* but not being quite certain about what such a thing should be. She could go and interrupt them, could speak to the girl about what she was doing and question whether she was being wise in her considerations, or she could do nothing and leave the girl to make up her own mind about such things. After all, she did not know who the girl was and certainly had no need to be so concerned for her.

But you know what it is like to have your reputation blackened, she reminded herself, wincing inwardly. *Can you not use that insight to prevent another from doing something so foolish?*

Her back straightened, her shoulders settling as Emma made her decision. Clearing her throat loudly, she approached the corner where Lord Rochester and the young lady stood, hearing the small exclamation that left the young lady's lips as she approached.

"Oh, good afternoon!" Emma said, loudly, as Lord Rochester turned in haste, blocking the view of the young lady behind him. "Lord Rochester. How... pleasant to see you." This was said with a good degree of irony that Emma could not keep from her voice. She saw the dark frown that lowered his brows and took in the way that his jaw set, his eyes flashing with evident anger. "And who is it that you are hiding behind you?" Taking a step forward, she forced Lord Rochester out of her way simply by moving ahead and saw a young lady of no more than seventeen standing there, her face ashen and her eyes flared with fright.

"And who might you be?" Emma asked, calmly, although inwardly her fury towards Lord Rochester was burning hotter than ever. "Are you engaged to Lord Rochester?"

Lord Rochester interrupted at once before the young lady could answer. "You need not speak to this young lady, Miss Bavidge," he told her firmly, putting one hand on her shoulder and attempting to tug her back. "She is in my care."

Emma turned swiftly, reached up, and wrenched Lord Rochester's hand from her shoulder. "That is precisely what concerns me, Lord Rochester," she stated, her heart beginning to quicken with both anger and fright over his foreboding presence. "Why is this young lady here with you alone if you are not engaged? Even if you *were* engaged, which I do not believe for a moment, her chaperone should still be nearby." She arched a brow and, with another long look towards Lord Rochester, turned back to the young lady, who was now a sickly green color.

"Miss...?"

The young lady closed her eyes tightly. "Miss Helen Jackson," she whispered, one hand reaching out towards Emma, trembling furiously as it did so. "Oh, I beg you, my lady, please..." Her words trailed off, her eyes begging Emma to remain silent about what she had just discovered, but Emma was not about to allow the young lady such a simple escape.

"Might I ask, Miss Jackson, why you are present here alone with a gentleman such as this?" she asked, keeping her voice gentle yet firm. "And where is your chaperone?"

"She—she is waiting outside in the carriage," Miss Jackson stammered, her whole body now trembling with fright. "My father has given me a companion as my mother is dead and my brother already married."

Emma shrugged. "Then why is she not within?" She watched the girl carefully, seeing how she looked up desperately towards Lord Rochester, clearly waiting for him to make some kind of explanation.

And then it dawned on her. Companions could, at times, be convinced to forgo their duties in some way if the right amount of money was paid. It was a paid position after all, and quite understandable that one might seek a little more income so long as nothing untoward happened to their charge. It would be rare for a companion to do such a thing but not entirely unheard of. It seemed that, in this case, this was precisely what had occurred.

Emma's anger burned furiously.

"I was only to stop inside for a few minutes," Miss Jackson whispered, her hands now pressed to her mouth as she shook her head wordlessly, her eyes brimming with tears. Her hands fell to her sides, her head falling forward as tears ran down her cheeks. "What have I done?"

"Thankfully, nothing as yet," Emma replied, grimly. "You have been discovered, yes, but that is only because I wished to ensure that you knew precisely what it is you are doing, Miss Jackson." Her brows hovered low over her eyes as she saw Miss Jackson look back at her. "You are about to ruin yourself for good, Miss Jackson. I can guarantee you that nothing Lord Rochester says to you about his affections and the like have any degree of truth to them." She threw a look towards Lord Rochester and saw just how dark his expression had become. "And you are about to give your reputation over to a gentleman who cares nothing for it and will care for you for however long pleases him. He will take from you without hesitation, Miss Jackson, but care nothing for the consequences. I can assure you of that."

Miss Jackson sniffed furiously and turned her gaze to Lord Rochester, a desperation in her eyes that, despite the circumstances, had Emma feeling terribly sorry for her. Lord Rochester was handsome, and even she herself knew that his words could be dripping with honey, appearing so honest and beguiling, when his heart itself was not true.

"Is that true, Lord Rochester?" Miss Jackson asked, her voice quavering. "Do you not care for me as you have said?"

Emma closed her eyes for a moment, sorry that the creature before her had been so taken in.

"I have told you the truth, Miss Jackson!" Lord Rochester protested at once, his eyes flaring wide. "You know very well that I care for you. Why else have I shown you such attentions?"

Emma restrained her snort of disbelief and, instead, arched an eyebrow. "Then, if it is as you say, Lord Rochester, I present to you a choice."

Lord Rochester's wide-eyed look of honesty faded to a simmering anger all over again, leaving Emma herself feeling rather tense and unsettled in his presence, but she still did not back down.

"A choice, Miss Bavidge?" Lord Rochester replied, his lip curling somewhat. "What choice might that be?"

"A simple one," Emma replied with a small shrug. "If you care for Miss Jackson here, as you say, then you will do the honorable thing and, this very moment, offer your hand in marriage." She looked calmly back at Lord Rochester, whose cheeks were now flaring red. "Since I have discovered you both in a rather delicate situation, it makes perfect sense for me to ask you this, does it not?" Having no response from Lord Rochester, she turned back to Miss Jackson, who was staring up desperately at Lord Rochester, clearly frantic for him to respond to her. "However, the opportunity is also presented for you to leave Miss Jackson's side and never return to her again, since I am willing to remain silent about what I have discovered." Tipping her head just a little, she looked back at Lord Rochester, who was grimacing as though in pain. "That is your choice, Lord Rochester. Either this very moment, offer your hand to Miss Jackson, or, if it is your preference, leave her side and never return to it again, knowing that this will bring with it my silence. It is up to you, Lord Rochester."

Emma's heart squeezed painfully at the look of hope in Miss Jackson's eyes. She watched the girl carefully, seeing how her face fell as Lord Rochester muttered something under his breath and, without hesitation, turned around to walk from the bookshop.

"This is not the end of our conversation, Miss Bavidge," Lord Rochester hissed, throwing a narrow-eyed glare towards her from over his shoulder. "I have a good deal more to say to you."

"But I am not inclined to hear it," Emma retorted, tossing her head and turning bodily away from him. "Good day, Lord Rochester."

The sound of the bell ringing as the door was pulled open seemed to be the last thing that Miss Jackson could cope with. She let out a shuddering breath and then pressed her hands to her eyes, clearly struggling to hold back the tears. Emma put one hand gently on the young lady's arm, knowing just how much regret the girl must be feeling.

"I am sorry, Miss Jackson," she said by way of apologizing for the difficulty the girl was going through, "but I do believe that it is for the best that you are fully aware of Lord Rochester and his malignant intentions." She pulled out a handkerchief and handed it to the girl, who took it at once, pressing it to her eyes. "Not all gentlemen are as he, Miss Jackson, although there is a good deal of them who would do all they could to take advantage in the same way that he has done. You must be on your guard."

A stifled sob came from the young lady, leaving Emma floundering, not quite certain what she should say or do to comfort Miss Jackson. Looking all about her, she was relieved to see Lady Smithton coming towards her, a look of concern etching itself into her features.

"Ah, Lady Smithton," Emma said, with relief. "Might you come and speak to Miss Jackson here? Are you acquainted with her?"

"I am not," Lady Smithton replied with a warm smile in Miss Jackson's direction, for she had just then removed the handkerchief from her eyes. "But I would be glad to offer any assistance you think would be helpful."

Briefly, Emma told Lady Smithton what had occurred, aware of just how shamed the young girl was. Lady Smithton nodded understandingly, not judging the girl and certainly making no comment about how foolish she had been to walk with Lord Rochester and leave her companion behind.

"I quite understand," Lady Smithton replied, her expression kind. "I shall speak to you for a few moments, Miss Jackson, if you will permit me? Thereafter, I intend to speak to that companion of yours, whomever she may be." Her smile faded as a look of anger and frustration entered her eyes. "We shall see you safely restored to the *beau monde* very soon, Miss Jackson, of course."

Miss Jackson sniffed, nodded, and dabbed at her eyes again, and Emma stepped out of the way, ensuring that Lady Smithton could make her way closer to the young lady. Her own heart was finally beginning to subdue itself, having been a little panicked by the furious way that Lord Rochester had looked at her. She did not know what he had meant by insisting that their conversation was not at an end and that he had some pertinent remarks which to press upon her, but Emma tried her best to simply dismiss the comments without considering them further. Lord Rochester had proven himself to be nothing but a rogue, hiding the truth of his character below a façade of honesty and consideration. How relieved she was that she had trusted Lord Morton's words! How glad that she had chosen to set Lord Rochester aside and, thereafter, accept the courtship of Lord Morton. The men were vastly different from each other and, in that, there came a sudden realization. The realization that she felt a good deal more than simple admiration and contentedness over her acquaintance with Lord Morton. There was a slow-growing fondness deep within her heart. It was so small that she did not want to give it a good deal of consideration, but even being aware of it seemed to bring a lightness to her spirit and a smile to her lips that spoke of a happy contentedness.

Suddenly, Emma could barely wait another moment until she saw him again. There was a good deal to tell him, but, more than that, she wanted to be within his presence and to look up into his eyes and to feel the fondness in her heart begin to grow and flourish until it became something entirely new and something utterly wonderful.

CHAPTER ELEVEN

*N*athaniel looked up in delight as Miss Bavidge walked into the room, her aunt beside her. She was dressed in a gown of blue, which he was certain would capture the color of her eyes and make her all the more lovely. Her aunt—a lady whom he had been introduced to but thought very bland—lifted her chin and turned her head away from her niece, walking into the room and leaving Miss Bavidge in her wake. Miss Bavidge did not appear to be affected by this in any way, for she merely shrugged and turned her head to the left and then to the right, evidently looking for someone.

A snake of excitement wriggled in his stomach as her eyes found him, for he bowed in greeting, seeing how her expression changed almost at once. Her smile grew steadily, and she quickly began to make her way towards him, dropping into a quick curtsy as she approached him.

"Good evening, Lord Morton," she said with a wry smile. "As you can see, I have been left to suffer this evening alone for my aunt is not inclined to spend much time with me." This was said without malice, as though it was something she had come to expect of her aunt. "I believe she continues to fear that my name alone will blemish her in some way even though the whispers about my father and myself have finally begun to fade!"

He grinned at her. "I am delighted to hear it!" he exclaimed, truly glad that she was no longer suffering as much. "Do you see the difference in the *beau monde*'s consideration of you, then?"

She shrugged one shoulder but smiled. "I can see that they do not always follow me with their eyes, nor whisper about me behind their hands," she replied, truthfully. "Although I believe that your attentions, as well as the efforts of Lord Havisham and Lady Smithton, have made the greatest difference. No longer am I bound to dance with those who will, thereafter, gossip about me to their companions, or who only seek my hand so as to achieve something their friends have also." Her expression tightened, but she still smiled. "Lord Havisham has been very careful with his introductions, for the most part." A chuckle escaped her, her eyes twinkling. "Although with Lord Rochester, I confess that I myself have surmised that he is not a gentleman of good character."

"No, he is not," Nathaniel replied, fervently, filled with relief that she had come to such a conclusion on her own. The night they had been in the theatre—which had been their first outing together—he had feared that Lord Rochester would seek her out to tell her the truth about what Nathaniel had done, but, thankfully, Miss Bavidge had been less than inclined to speak to him. That did not mean that Nathaniel had any less responsibility when it came to telling Miss Bavidge the truth but, as yet, no opportunity had presented itself.

He winced inwardly, feeling a stab of guilt. That was not quite the truth, of course, for he had enjoyed a good many times with Miss Bavidge over the last fortnight that he could have used to be honest with her about her father and his involvement in the affair, but each time he had chosen not to do so. He had told himself that it was not the right time, that he would ruin the time they had shared thus far if he spoke to her of it, and so had shied away from doing what he must.

Another stab of guilt pushed hard into his heart, but with an effort, Nathaniel ignored it. There would be a right time; he was sure of it. There was no great hurry for him to speak to Miss Bavidge about it, for ever since she had turned her head away from Lord Rochester, he had known that she would not be giving the gentleman any great length of time with which to speak.

"I am glad to see you here this evening, Miss Bavidge," he said, feeling a great swell in his heart that sent his mind into a sudden flurry of thoughts and emotions. "You look quite lovely."

At this, Miss Bavidge blushed prettily, turning her head away just a little. She was unused to such compliments, which made Nathaniel all the more eager to give them.

"Your gown captures the color of your eyes," he continued a little more softly so that they would not be overheard by any of the other guests. "They remind me of the sea, of the crashing waves that break on the shore."

Miss Bavidge's cheeks were still warm, but she looked

up at him in interest. "You have been to the sea?" she asked, sounding excited. "Truly?"

"Truly," he replied, with a grin. "And it was quite a remarkable experience, I must say."

Miss Bavidge clasped her hands together, a look of longing etching itself onto her face. "I should love to see such a sight," she said with such a fervency that Nathaniel could not help but feel a sudden urge to scoop her up in his arms and take her to the sea at once, even though it was a great distance away! "It must have been quite wonderful."

"Quite," Nathaniel replied a little thickly, as he struggled to comprehend all that he was feeling. "As I look into your face, I am transported back there, Miss Bavidge. It was—and is—quite a lovely sight."

"You are very kind, Lord Morton," Miss Bavidge replied, with a small smile in his direction, her cheeks still flushed. "Tell me, is there anywhere else that you have been or that you wish to go to still?"

Nathaniel considered this and, for a time, the two of them fell into conversation about such things. It continually surprised him just how easy it was to talk to Miss Bavidge, how open and willing she was to listen to him. She was intelligent and bright, with a sharp wit that often made him laugh aloud. There was an ease in her manner that warmed his heart, making it almost a joy to converse with her, and for this, Nathaniel was truly grateful. There was something about her that he could not turn away from, something that was steadily growing within his heart that he did not want to ignore.

Something so profound that, if he allowed it, would fill his whole being.

"This evening appears to be rather dull thus far," Miss Bavidge commented, suddenly, her voice so quiet that he had to strain to hear it. "I do not know Lord Langton well, but this affair does not seem to be particularly exciting."

Nathaniel chuckled, looking all about him. Lord Langton was an older gentleman who had married a younger wife and, therefore, was now required to throw such soirees so as to please her. No doubt Lady Langton would soon announce that she was to perform a few pieces on the pianoforte, which would be accompanied by her *'dear'* sister, who was still unmarried, and therefore pushed forward by Lady Langton at almost every opportunity. The problem was, of course, that Lady Langton did not play the pianoforte particularly well and her sister, also, did not sing with any degree of accomplishment.

"I have been to these gatherings on a few prior occasions," he told Miss Bavidge, his gaze suddenly catching sight of Lady Langton, who had drawn near to her husband and was whispering frantically in his ear. "If you wish to be saved from an hour of tedious entertainment, might I suggest that we take a short walk about the gardens? It is light enough still outside that we may be seen and the lanterns are sure to be lit."

Miss Bavidge frowned, however, not immediately accepting his offer. "I would be glad to," she said, slowly, not quite catching his eye. "But I should like to take a companion with me."

He looked back at her steadily, wondering why she had turned down a few minutes alone with him. "If you wish," he agreed at once, feeling a sudden sense of disappointment flood him as though her request for them to be accompanied had frustrated him in some way. "Is Lady Smithton present?"

Miss Bavidge shook her head, looking about her in evident frustration. "My aunt is the only one present at this time," she replied as Lady Langton made to make her way towards the pianoforte. Biting her lip, Miss Bavidge glanced back at him, now appearing a little uncertain. "Mayhap if we stayed within the view of the rest of the guests?"

"Miss Bavidge." Surprised by her apparent concern, Nathaniel took a small step forward, reaching out for her hand, which she gave with only a momentary hesitation. "Miss Bavidge, you have nothing to fear from me," he promised her. "I shall not attempt to press my advantage nor do anything untoward. I assure you of that. All I seek to do is remove both yourself and myself from what will soon become a fairly unpleasant situation." Smiling at her, he glanced to his left and saw a few guests suddenly hurrying towards the French doors, with one throwing a glance towards Lady Langton as she seated herself at the pianoforte. Chuckling, he gestured to them. "It seems we will not be alone in any way, Miss Bavidge, for there are clearly others who wish to do the same!" He watched in amusement as Miss Bavidge looked towards where he gestured, seeing the surprise and then the tinge of mirth appear in her expression.

"If you please, if you please!" Lord Langton was

speaking loudly now, trying to garner the attention of his guests, and this seemed to spur Miss Bavidge into action. She pulled her hand from his and set it quickly on his arm, throwing a darting glance behind her to where Lord Langton was still speaking. Nathaniel did not hesitate but hurried her towards the French doors, only just making it out of doors before Lord Langton asked his guests to seat themselves so that they might listen to his wife's performance.

"That is something of a relief," Nathaniel chuckled as Miss Bavidge looked up into his face. "You do not know how many times I have had to endure such a thing as this!" Recalling the last time, he let out a small groan, running one hand down over his face. "It was quite torturous the last time, and yet I was still expected to make out that I enjoyed every moment."

"Then I suppose I should be glad that you have rescued me," Miss Bavidge replied with a look of relief and a twinkle of delight back in her eyes, her anxiety gone. "And it seems you are not the only one to have made such an escape."

Nathaniel looked out towards the rest of the gardens, seeing at least fifteen others who had done the very same. The evening was light still, with the sun seeming to refuse to set, and he could make the guests out without any great difficulty. "Indeed, Miss Bavidge," he replied with a broad smile. "You are quite right. Although I am sorry if I pushed you into attending with me. If you do not feel comfortable walking in the gardens, then I must apologize."

"There is nothing to apologize for, Lord Morton,"

Miss Bavidge replied quickly. "Please, do not concern yourself." She cleared her throat gently but looked away. "I confess it is only because of something that occurred recently that gives me a twist of concern which, I know for certain, I need not have with you." Quickly, she told him what she had seen of Lord Rochester in the bookshop and how she had come to the aid of a young lady, and Nathaniel felt his anger begin to burn deep within him. "I suppose I have become overly wary, although my heart knows that I need have no concern over your presence here with me."

"No, indeed not, Miss Bavidge," Nathaniel replied fervently, wanting to reassure her. "I would never press my advantage in such a way, and I pray that you know that the words I speak are from my heart, and certainly are not a mask by which I hide my true intentions."

Something seemed to spark in the air between them as Miss Bavidge looked up into his eyes, their steps slowing. "I do know that, truly," Miss Bavidge answered quietly, her hand tightening on his arm. "I should not have allowed myself to be so concerned, Lord Morton. I know the kind of gentleman you are, and for that, I am truly grateful. You have helped me to remove myself from the pit of darkness and despair that I had fallen into from the very first day I returned to society."

"I am glad that I was of some assistance," he replied, but Miss Bavidge was not yet finished. She held up one hand, and Nathaniel turned to face her a little more, aware that they had strayed a little off the garden path.

"Your consideration of me when I did not even know your name has struck me time and again," Miss Bavidge continued softly, her free hand now pressed lightly against his chest. "You knew of my distress, and you wished to aid me in some way. That kindness is something that is lacking a good many gentlemen, Lord Morton, and I feel blessed by God in heaven for your kindness and your good company these last few days." Her voice was still soft, her expression still gentle, but her eyes were burning orbs, fixed upon his until he could feel the heat of the fire that burned within her. "Your character evidences itself in all that you do and all that you are," she told him, pausing only to swallow hard, as though overcome with her own emotions. "I have found myself recently looking forward to seeing you again, Lord Morton, as if I cannot be satisfied with one day's activities or visits." A slight blush tinged her cheeks, but she did not stop speaking. "I will be honest with you, Lord Morton, as you have been with me. I struggle to know all that I feel and all that I hope for since these emotions are greater than any I have ever considered before."

This was something of a revelation, and Nathaniel felt his mouth go dry, looking down into her face and seeing the hope flickering there. She had spoken to him with a bold honesty that revealed her very heart and, in doing so, had rendered him practically speechless. To have gone from an unwillingness even to walk with him in the gardens to now be speaking to him in such an intimate manner was quite astonishing. Had she simply realized that what she feared would never come to pass and so, in realizing that, had felt the urge to speak to him about what filled her heart? It was both astonishing and overwhelming, flooding him with an appreciation for her that burned its way into his heart.

"You have said nothing for some moments, Lord Morton," Miss Bavidge said, stammering just a little as she dropped her gaze to the ground. "I do hope I have not upset you or spoken out of turn."

"No, no indeed," he replied at once, with such a fervency that Miss Bavidge looked back up at him immediately. "It is just that I am a little surprised; that is all."

"Oh." Miss Bavidge did not look pleased by such a remark, for no smile stretched her lips, and no joy leaped into her eyes. Instead, she merely stood and waited a little longer, her hand dropping from where it had rested against him.

Nathaniel caught it at once, his fingers warm against hers as he continued to search her face. He did not know what it was that he felt and certainly could not imagine trying to put it into any sort of coherent sentence, but at the same time, he did not want Miss Bavidge to feel as though he thought her expression of respect and apparent affection to have been less than worthwhile.

"I..." Closing his eyes for a moment, Nathaniel took in a long breath and forced himself to be honest, in much the same way as she had done. "I will not pretend that I have no feelings for you, Miss Bavidge. I look forward to your company. In fact, I relish it." This, he saw, brought a smile to her face, and that, in turn, filled his heart with a relief that he could not turn away from. "I have sought to court you, and I have been glad to do so this last fortnight. There is no intention in my heart to bring our courtship to an end, Miss Bavidge, for I find there is something between us that goes beyond a mere acquaintance."

"Indeed," Miss Bavidge answered, her expression now one of relief. "I feel that also."

"But," Nathaniel continued, the words sticking to his throat as he thought again of what he had done to bring Miss Bavidge's father to his untimely departure from society. "But there is something I must speak to you of, Miss Bavidge. Something I must tell you before I can even consider my intentions for this courtship."

Miss Bavidge frowned hard, her smile gone in a trice, and Nathaniel felt his heart twist in his chest. He wanted to be honest with her and this, it seemed, was the very time to do it. However, try as he might, the words would not come to him. He did not even know what to say to begin such a conversation, for, with the look in Miss Bavidge's eyes and the awareness of just how closely she stood to him, Nathaniel could think of nothing else.

"Miss Bavidge, I—"

Before he could say anything more, Miss Bavidge surprised him utterly by reaching up and pressing her mouth to his. Astonished, Nathaniel pulled back at once, seeing the heat flare in her cheeks as he took a step away from her.

"I—I must apologize, Lord Morton," Miss Bavidge stammered, turning away from him at once and pressing a hand to her mouth. "I had no intention of doing such a thing nor of being so forward, particularly when I had such a fear of the very same coming from you." Wincing, she pressed her hand to her forehead, clearly regretting what she had done. "Forgive me."

She wasn't looking at him, clearly too ashamed to bring her eyes to his. Nathaniel remained utterly stunned, his mouth burning from where she had kissed him and his heart so thunderous that he could barely hear what she had said. His mind was swimming, his thoughts tumbling over one another like a waterfall. And yet, all through it came the fierce desire to do just the very same again.

"Please, Miss Bavidge." His hand reached out to her as Nathaniel slowly became aware of the dim light that surrounded them now as the sun began to fade away and the lantern light started to glow. "You need not apologize, truly. It is only that you took me quite by surprise."

Miss Bavidge said nothing but dropped her head low as she turned back to him. Her cheeks were a vicious scarlet but, as he watched her, Nathaniel felt a sudden urge to laugh bubbling up in him. She had behaved in the very way she had feared he might, clearly overcome with the emotions and desires that had been running through her heart, and he could not hold her to account for that.

"Please, Miss Bavidge, do not look away from me," he coaxed, seeing how her gaze slowly began to rise. "You have nothing to fear. I will not berate you, nor will I hold you in disdain. I quite understand what you did and why you did such a thing."

"You do?" Miss Bavidge looked up at him sharply, her eyes wide in surprise.

"Of course." Unable to prevent himself, Nathaniel reached out and gently grasped her chin, feeling the softness of her skin under his fingers and feeling the sparks shoot up his arm. "It is a desire that has been growing within my own heart for some time, although I have not ever thought to pursue it, such has been my concern for you." He chuckled as Miss Bavidge looked away again. "But now that I know that you feel much the same way, I shall not hold myself back the next time such a desire comes upon me."

"Then you shall spare my blushes," Miss Bavidge replied, trying to laugh but still clearly mortified. "Only say that you will give me your forgiveness, Lord Morton, for without it, I shall remain utterly ashamed of myself."

Leaning forward, Nathaniel pressed his lips to Miss Bavidge's forehead for just a moment, praying that no other guest would be able to make them out in the dim light. "You have nothing to seek forgiveness for, Miss Bavidge," he told her, softly. "Do not fret any longer." The urge to lean down and kiss her again, but for much longer this time, burned hot within him and it took a good deal of effort for Nathaniel to step away, offering her his arm as he had done before.

"Thank you, Lord Morton," Miss Bavidge murmured, accepting his arm at once and falling into step alongside him. "Although I fear that my embarrassment shall remain for some time, even with your assurances!"

He chuckled, reached across, and patted her hand. "Be that as it may, Miss Bavidge, I still fully intend to pursue our courtship without hesitation. You have done nothing other than satisfy the questions in my mind regarding our courtship." Glancing down at her, he saw Miss Bavidge smile and felt his lips curve in response. "I look forward to our next walk together, Miss Bavidge."

She laughed at this and Nathaniel chuckled with her,

pushing out of his mind the knowledge that he had, yet again, turned from speaking the truth to her. The kiss, whilst surprising, had not been a reason to remain silent about matters with her father, but he had chosen to push it aside again. Telling himself that he would do so tomorrow, when they walked in the park, Nathaniel turned Miss Bavidge back towards the path, and they began to wander along it together, safe and secure in each other's company.

CHAPTER TWELVE

"What did you do, Emma?"

Emma blushed furiously but did not look at her friend, Miss Crosby. "Nothing improper," she lied, knowing full well that this was precisely what she had done. "I am becoming aware that Lord Morton is becoming very dear to me, I will admit," she said, honestly, aware of Miss Crosby's astonished look. "I am aware that it has been a fortnight since we started courting and I myself am astonished that I feel such strength of emotion, but I have been with the gentleman almost every day, and my heart has certainly changed significantly in that time."

Miss Crosby sighed softly, her eyes gentle. "That sounds quite lovely, Emma. I am truly glad for you."

"But it has been so swift!" Emma protested, feeling a little uncertain that what she felt could be so real after such a short length of time. "I never expected to have such strong emotions for a gentleman, I confess it. Whilst

I hoped that Lady Smithton might be able to guide me to a suitable gentleman, I never gave any thought to having affection between oneself and one's husband." She shook her head, still not quite certain that this was happening to her. "Can it be true?"

"Indeed, it can."

Emma jumped in surprise and then looked towards the door, seeing Lady Smithton standing there, laughter in her eyes.

"I *do* apologize for interrupting your private conversation," Lady Smithton said, coming further into the room. "But I could not help but overhear." She smiled and sat down on a chair between Emma and Miss Crosby. "You have an affection for Lord Morton then, do you?"

Nodding, Emma laced her fingers together and dropped her gaze, still very embarrassed to even admit to such a thing. "I confess that it has been tormenting my mind for some days, Lady Smithton," she answered truthfully. "I find Lord Morton to be kind, generous, and considerate in almost every way. We have excellent conversation for he is both sharp-witted and intelligent. However, he does not treat me as though I have no intelligence of my own either." Pausing, she recalled how he had complimented her only two days ago at the rather lackluster event held by Lord Langton, remarking on the shade of her eyes and how they reminded her of the sea. She had been more affected by that remark than he knew. "He speaks well of me and, I believe, has some fondness for me also, which I cannot pretend does not lighten my spirits." Swallowing, she looked away again, still struggling to speak of such intimate feelings openly. "Therefore, I must confess that I have an affection for him within my heart. Quite what I am to do with it, I have very little idea for it is overwhelming even to become aware of it!"

Lady Smithton beamed at her, her eyes dancing with happiness. "You need do nothing to it, my dear, other than nurture it," she replied with a soft smile. "If it is returned, as you believe it to be, then why do you fear it? There is nothing that need confuse you, for it is quite natural to have such feelings."

"But they have come so swiftly!" Emma protested, her fear gnawing at her. Fear that she was feeling too much and much too quickly also. "I am overcome by the love I feel at times, Lady Smithton."

Lady Smithton smiled and shook her head. "I am here to guide and reassure you, am I not?" she asked, gently. "Then be assured that your emotions are quite natural. They may overwhelm you, they may swirl about you in a most tempestuous fashion, but that is just what they do. In time, they will settle and begin to flood you with the most wonderful of sensations. They will be content to grow steadily and bring brightness to your life that you have not known before."

Emma accepted this but frowned just a little upon seeing the way Lady Smithton spoke, for it was with a gentle wistfulness that seemed to speak of a deep understanding of love and how it affected a person. Emma did not think that Lady Smithton had ever loved her late husband, for, by all accounts, he had been a good deal older than she and had possessed a character of great darkness also. Who then could have sparked such feelings within Lady Smithton's heart? Her mind turned back to Lord Havisham, aware of just how much he seemed to admire Lady Smithton but also how she kept him a little apart from her. Could it be that Lady Smithton had, at one time, loved Lord Havisham? Or that she felt such things for him now but, for whatever reason, set them aside from herself?

"Do you believe that Lord Morton has the best of intentions for you?" Lady Smithton asked, dragging Emma's attention from her own questions. "Do you believe that he will soon ask for your hand?"

Another swirl of emotion clogged up Emma's heart, making it difficult for her to catch her breath. Lord Morton had not been specific as yet, but her certainty that he would do as Lady Smithton had suggested began to grow within her heart.

"Yes, I do," she said, seeing Lady Smithton nod again. "I think that to be most likely."

"Then mayhap I should speak to him," Lady Smithton murmured, tilting her head and regarding Emma carefully. "To ensure that his intentions are as you believe them to be."

Emma shook her head, appreciative of Lady Smithton's willingness to help but feeling a sense of protectiveness over what was her blossoming acquaintance with Lord Morton. "I appreciate your offer of help, truly," she stammered, hoping she was not offending the lady. "But I confess that I consider this to be something I can manage on my own. Although," she added, with a small laugh, "I have needed your guidance to surmise that my feelings are entirely as they ought to be!"

Miss Crosby laughed also, leaning forward in her chair and catching Emma's eye. "Then mayhap, very soon, you shall be the first of 'The Spinsters Guild' to find themselves engaged!" she exclaimed, sending a sudden thrill down Emma's spine. "And just how delighted we shall all be for you. You shall give us hope!"

Emma smiled back at her friend, aware of how Miss Crosby spoke with a slight twinge of envy in her voice. "I am certain that with Lady Smithton's guidance, you shall all find happiness," she replied, trying to put as much certainty into her voice as she could. "I am grateful indeed for your help, Lady Smithton, and for the guidance of Lord Havisham also."

"Although it seems you have not needed a great deal of my input, given that a gentleman was already pursuing you," Lady Smithton replied with a smile in her voice. "Lord Morton just needed to become aware of his feelings regarding you, I think." Her expression suddenly became a little more serious. "You do feel as though you can trust him, however?"

Emma considered this, recalling all the strange conversations she had needed to have with Lord Morton. "I think that I understand why he wished to keep me away from Lord Rochester," she answered slowly, thinking through everything. "I also consider him to have a kind heart, given his awareness of my difficult situation in re-entering society." She hesitated, suddenly realizing that she did not quite understand everything, which sent a flurry of discontent through her. "I know that he had a falling out with Lord Rochester, which explains why Lord Rochester himself seemed so willing to throw falseness about Lord Morton towards me, but I still do not understand why he could not speak openly to me about his concerns over Lord Rochester at the first." This made her frown all the more, recalling how he had seemed so reluctant, only to speak a good deal more openly sometime later. "That does seem somewhat strange."

"But is it enough to concern you?" Lady Smithton asked quietly. "Or will you simply leave it be?"

Emma hesitated, working through the tangles of her mind. "I am not quite certain," she replied slowly. "I think I shall have to speak to Lord Morton of it again before I will be completely satisfied. It is not in my nature to leave a matter of uncertainty to such confusion."

"I well understand that," Lady Smithton said as Miss Crosby nodded her agreement. "Then may I suggest that, before he takes matters any further, you speak honestly to Lord Morton about what has just come to your mind." She lifted one shoulder in a half shrug. "It may be that there is a very simple explanation."

"Such as, he did not know you well enough initially to speak honestly about his broken friendship with Lord Rochester," Miss Crosby suggested as Lady Smithton got up to ring the bell for tea. "That would make complete sense."

"Indeed it would," Emma agreed, her uneasiness disappearing swiftly as she realized that her friends both spoke wisdom. "In fact, Sarah, I believe you are quite right." Straightening her shoulders, Emma turned back to Lady Smithton, wanting to change the subject of conversation to other, less weighty matters. "And might I ask if any of the other young ladies within 'The Spinsters Guild' are as I am?"

Lady Smithton laughed, straightening her skirts as she sat back down. "You shall have to ask Miss Crosby about such a thing, I think," she replied, giving Miss Crosby a knowing look. "For being supposed spinsters, each of you ladies has more than enough gentlemen within their reach!"

With wide eyes, Emma turned back to look at her friend, seeing how Miss Crosby blushed furiously, turning her head away to hide it from Emma.

"Sarah!" Emma exclaimed, half laughing, half astonished. "What is it that you are hiding from me?"

Miss Crosby turned around and was about to answer, only for the door to open and the maid to step in with a tea tray.

"I think you should wait for a time, Miss Crosby, until tea has been served," Lady Smithton advised with a broad smile. "It will give you a few minutes to collect yourself—although I do not think you have anything to fear from telling Miss Bavidge the truth."

Miss Crosby glanced back at Sarah and blushed again but nodded. "That is true," she agreed quietly. "But let us wait until we have each a teacup and saucer prepared, for mayhap by then, my blushes will have faded!"

This made Emma laugh, the last remnants of concern and fright fading away from her as she saw her friend smile. A happiness filled her heart as Lady Smithton began to pour the tea: a happiness that was not only for her but for her friend also. She hoped desperately that Miss Crosby would find a joy in her own life in the same way Emma was beginning to discover one in her own. It was truly the most astonishing and delightful experience Emma thought she could ever have the blessing to discover.

Walking to the bookshop on her way back to her aunt's, Emma was glad that she had chosen to walk instead of taking a hackney. Lady Smithton had, of course, offered the carriage, but Emma had refused it, thinking that the afternoon was fine and that she would have more than enough time to prepare for the ball that evening by the time she got back home. Her aunt, of course, had sniffed indelicately when Emma had told her that Lord Morton would be seeking her company out specifically at the ball, although she had made some comment about how Emma's father would be delighted to hear of just how successful her aunt's endeavors on Emma's behalf had been. The fact that the ball was being thrown by Lord Knighton, the man who had almost been blackmailed by Emma's father, had not gone unnoticed by both Emma and her aunt, however. It appeared that Lord Knighton was willing to set things aside regarding Emma, at least, and for that, she was very grateful. However, she was also quite certain that Lord Morton had involved himself a great deal in the matter of garnering her an invitation.

Not that her aunt had been pleased or grateful for such a kindness!

Trying not to roll her eyes at the memory of this, Emma continued to make her way towards the bookshop, recalling what had occurred the last time she had stepped within. She hoped that Miss Jackson had not allowed the occurrence to affect her too greatly, although, at the same time, she prayed that the girl would know better than to accept the invitation of a handsome gentleman without any consideration for propriety or her own reputation.

"Ah, Miss Bavidge. Finally, I am to have the opportunity to speak to you."

She whirled about, seeing her maid staggering back as a gentleman thrust her aside, taking long strides towards Emma. A scream lodged in her throat at the malevolent figure of Lord Rochester, seeing just how furious he appeared to be, although she had no explicable reason as to why that might be.

"I have no wish to speak to you, Lord Rochester," she told him firmly, making to turn around and continue on her way, only to feel his hand clamping down on her shoulder, his fingers vice-like. Pain screamed through her, but she remained as she was with an effort, refusing to turn back to him.

"Remove your hand from me, Lord Rochester," she stated, firmly, even though her heart was thundering furiously within her chest. "How dare you behave in such a manner!"

This, much to her relief, seemed to have the effect she had been hoping for, given that Lord Rochester did remove his hand at once—only for him to come directly in front of her, stepping into her path.

"I have tried and tried again to speak to you, Miss Bavidge, but you have either dodged me or ensured that I am unable to do so," he stated, his brows so low that all she could see were dark shadows were his eyes should have been. "You have done so purposefully."

Emma, as frightened as she was, became aware that there were other passers-by near to them and so, knowing that he would not place a hand on her again for fear of what might occur, drew herself up with as much confidence as she could.

"I have avoided you entirely, Lord Rochester," she stated, honestly. "I have no wish to speak to you, nor have I had any desire to further our acquaintance. I believe you are fully aware of this." She arched one eyebrow, challenging him to refute her claim, but he did not. "Therefore, I cannot understand why you appear to feel so troubled towards me when I have made it clear that I do not wish to converse with you!"

"Lord Morton has told you lies," he began, only for Emma to hold up one hand, silencing him. He was clearly shocked by her confidence, which gave rise to yet more assurance within her heart.

"I know that Lord Morton spoke to you of a particular matter and begged you to keep it secret," she answered, seeing Lord Rochester's jaw work hard. "But you did not. The trust of friendship was broken. Therefore, he has chosen to stay apart from you, and you, in turn, have sought to disparage him."

Lord Rochester laughed harshly, his tone hard and grating, and Emma felt herself wince.

"You may believe that you know the truth of the matter, Miss Bavidge, but have you ever questioned what matter it was that Lord Morton discussed with me?" he asked, his glare sending a shiver down her spine. "Have you not questioned why he seemed so unwilling to tell you his reasons for asking you to keep away from me?" He laughed again, the sound setting Emma's teeth on edge. "Oh, he took a great risk in telling you what he did, but you believed his words and, thereafter, decided to turn your back on me. I have sought to do what I threatened, but your aloofness and judgment have kept you from hearing the truth from my lips."

Revulsion, mingled with fear, began to snake through Emma's heart. "I have no wish to hear any supposed *truth* from your lips, Lord Rochester," she stated, as calmly as she could. "Now, if you will excuse me, I—"

"Not even when it concerns your father?"

The words seemed to split the air between them, rendering Emma entirely silent with shock and horror. She could not help but stare at Lord Rochester, seeing how he was grinning at her with the arrogance of a gentleman who knew that he has said something injurious and inflammatory in equal measure.

"I do not know to what you are referring, Lord Rochester," Emma managed to say, her lips seeming to stick together as she tried to speak in a clear and confident manner. "Now, if you will excuse me, I—"

"Who do you think brought your father's deeds into the light?" Lord Rochester asked, taking a step closer to her and narrowing his gaze, his lips a thin red slash across his face, his jaw jutting forward.

Emma closed her eyes, her breath shuddering out of her. "I am certain that I—"

"Someone knew of it, did they not?" Lord Rochester continued, silencing her. "Someone spoke of it to another and then another and then another, until the word spread about your father's disgrace." His lip curled, his eyes narrowing even further. "Someone told the *beau monde* of your father's disgrace, and, in doing so, condemned you to your fate. They could have kept their knowledge close, could have told only those who were required to know of it, but they did not. They told everyone they knew, ensuring that the rumor mills began to work quickly and with great efficiency." His breath was putrid as he leaned even closer, his presence blocking out everything else around her. "And I think, Miss Bavidge, that you need to ask yourself who would do such a thing, and why."

Emma wanted to reach out and push Lord Rochester away, wanted to push him from her vision and from her mind, but his words had dug too deeply into her thoughts and began to bury their way into her heart. She could barely breathe, for her breaths were shallow and hasty, her eyes blinking up at the gentleman before her who now stood there, his gaze calculating.

She was numb. Her fingers were cold, her limbs frozen in place. She knew precisely what Lord Rochester was suggesting but did not want to believe it. It could not be that *he* was the one who had spoken of her father's behavior to the *beau monde*, surely? It had never once been a question in her mind before this moment, for she had simply presumed that word had got out somehow and that attempting to find the person responsible was both futile and without merit.

However, if what Lord Rochester stated was true, then it meant that Lord Morton had not simply been seeking her out due to his knowledge of what she had to endure. It was because he knew precisely what would occur for her return, given that he had been the one responsible for spreading the story about.

Lord Rochester cannot be trusted.

A small whisper entered her head, just as her world began to spin about her. Could she really trust what Lord Rochester was saying? He who had been seen with Miss Jackson in such an inappropriate manner? It did not seem as though he were the sort of man she could trust implicitly, yet his words did raise a question in her mind. Questions that she needed to answer.

"Lord Morton told me that you were once friends," she whispered, wobbling slightly on her feet as she spoke to Lord Rochester. "That you betrayed him."

Lord Rochester scoffed, his face ugly. "I told him not to speak to anyone else about what he had discovered, but he did not listen to me. He might wish to blame me for that, but I will not accept it from him."

Emma shook her head, a vision of Lord Morton filling her mind as she did so. He was a gentleman who had spoken such gentle and comforting words to her that she could not immediately believe that he was a liar. He had not behaved cruelly towards her but had rather shown compassion.

I have no ill will towards you.

The words once spoken by Lord Morton ran through her mind again, steadying her somewhat. "I do not believe you," she stated as firmly as she could even though her mind was racing. "I cannot accept it from you, Lord Rochester."

"Of course you do not," Lord Rochester replied, irony in his voice. "Then I shall leave you to decide whether or not you wish to discuss the matter further with Lord Morton himself. Otherwise..." He shrugged and made to turn away, only to look back at her. "You might wonder, mayhap, why you do not know of this from Lord Morton's own lips, Miss Bavidge. Why has he not told you that he was the one who discovered your father's intention to blackmail the Earl of Knighton? Could it be that he is ashamed of what he has done?" A smirk tugged at one corner of his mouth, making Emma shudder violently. "Mayhap, you should ask, Miss Bavidge, why a gentleman should hide such a thing from his young lady if he feels no guilt or distress over it? What is it, Miss Bavidge, that your Lord Morton is trying to hide from you?" With this question, he straightened his hat, gave her a quick, jerky nod, and strode away from her.

Emma blinked rapidly, feeling a fog closing in about her. Struggling to breathe, struggling even to stay upright, she had to fight for every moment, strive for every breath until, finally, she felt it begin to clear.

No, her mind screamed, *no, it cannot be true. Lord Morton would not hide such a thing from me.* The rational part of her wanted to try to find an excuse for him, wanted to make her see that, should he have had a part in revealing the depths of her father's mistakes, then he had every reason to be afraid of speaking to her of it. However, she could not be that rational, not when she feared that there was more truth to Lord Rochester's explanations. If Lord Morton had spoken to others in the *ton* about what he knew, then it would explain why he had watched for her during her first few weeks of the season. Perhaps it had been a way of assuaging his guilt.

"And he did not tell me precisely why he was afraid to talk to me about Lord Rochester," she said aloud, her heart still pounding furiously as blood roared in her ears. When she had asked him, he had prevaricated for a prolonged length of time and had only spoken the truth— or as much of the truth as he had been willing to share with her—when she had insisted that he do so. The outcome of which had been that she had set her mind against Lord Rochester and had determined not to even speak a word to him unless she was forced to. Had she not even written a note to Lord Rochester, informing him that she had forgotten another social engagement as a way to escape his request to take her to the theatre? Perhaps Lord Morton had breathed a sigh of relief when she had agreed to be accompanied by him instead of by Lord Rochester. Perhaps none of what he said he felt for her was true.

This thought brought a sudden swell of pain to her chest, leaving her eyes blinking back tears. It did not make sense, given that Lord Morton had been so attentive to her of late, for surely if he had been attempting to ensure that she never discovered the truth, he would have done his best to stay away from her? None of it seemed to make any sense, and question upon question began to stack on top of each other in the depths of her mind. Stumbling forward, Emma attempted to make her way home without revealing the agony that ravaged her soul to any other passer-by. Her steps were heavy, her arms hanging down by her sides as even a sliver of peace refused to come to her. All she felt was pain and confusion, her heart broken, and her mind tormented.

Just what was it Lord Morton had done?

CHAPTER THIRTEEN

"This one, I think."

Nathaniel looked down at the beautiful silver pendant that lay in the silk-lined box and felt certain that this one would do perfectly for Miss Bavidge. Waiting until the gentleman on the other side of the counter had pulled it from the box and handed it to him for inspection, Nathaniel held it carefully, examining it from every angle.

The pendant was quite lovely, with a single blue sapphire in the center surrounded by a delicate silver. It was not too heavy and certainly not too gaudy, and he was quite confident that it would suit Miss Bavidge very well indeed. It would bring out the color of her eyes: eyes that he could barely forget for even a moment.

"Yes, thank you," he told the shopkeeper, who looked delighted that he had made such an excellent sale. "If you would wrap it, then I should like to purchase it at once."

The shopkeeper bowed and murmured something,

taking the pendant back from Nathaniel and replacing it in the box. Leaving the fellow to do his work, Nathaniel continued to look around the shop, although his mind was not at all fixed on the many jewels that were displayed. Instead, they were fixed on one person alone: Miss Emma Bavidge.

Tonight's ball was to be a rather splendid affair, given that it was hosted by the Earl of Knighton himself. The earl who had been saved from being blackmailed by Miss Bavidge's now disgraced father now considered Nathaniel a great friend and had, of course, invited him to the ball without hesitation. However, it had come as something of a surprise when Nathaniel had begged an invitation for Miss Bavidge also. However, as gracious as he was, the Earl had considered what Nathaniel had said and thus had done as he had asked. An invitation had been issued, and Nathaniel was glad to know that Emma had accepted. It would be an excellent evening, Nathaniel was certain, for it would show the *beau monde* that the Earl himself had set matters between himself and Miss Bavidge aside, which Nathaniel hoped would bring an end to the whispers that continued to dog her, albeit less of them of late. It would be made all the more wonderful if Nathaniel was able to do as he intended and asked Miss Bavidge to marry him.

Ever since Miss Bavidge had kissed him so unexpectedly, Nathaniel had been unable to forget that moment. The softness of her lips, the astonishment in her eyes at her actions, and the words spoken thereafter had refused to leave him. He had awoken at night, his first thought one of her, and thus, he had been convinced that the urgent desire in his heart had to be satisfied in the only way he could think. He had to ask Miss Bavidge to marry him and pray that, with his confession given to her about the role he had played in father's downfall, she still might accept him. There was no doubt in Nathaniel's mind that he had to be nothing but honest. Every word he spoke had to be the truth. He would tell her why he had not spoken to her of it before, be open about his guilt and his confusion. In vulnerability, he would set everything else aside and open up his heart to her scrutiny.

He could only pray he had not done her too much of a wrong in keeping his confession so hidden for so long.

"My lord?"

Tugged out of his thoughts and desires, Nathaniel turned back to the shopkeeper, who was standing with the package in his hand. Paying for the pendant, he pocketed it quickly, and then left the shop.

The street was fairly busy, but Nathaniel had no intention of lingering. There was nothing else he needed to do here at present, for he had secured what he needed and therefore did not need to remain. The ball would soon be in full swing, and he would need to return home to wash and change. He hoped that Miss Bavidge's presence at the ball would make the *beau monde* cease their whisperings about her and her father, although he was certain that offering her his hand in marriage would, in its own way, bring about a good many whisperings! Smiling to himself, Nathaniel strode down the pavement, looking for his carriage, which he had left a short distance away.

"Lord Morton!"

A familiar voice caught his ears and he turned around to see none other than Lady Smithton and Lord Havisham walking together down the street. Lady Smithton's sharp eyes were taking him in, as they always did, although her smile was warm. Lord Havisham was grinning his welcome, although that might well have come from the fact that Lady Smithton had her hand on his arm and was walking in step with him. The gentleman was clearly delighted that he had such a fine partner, and that in itself made Nathaniel smile.

"Good afternoon, Lady Smithton, Lord Havisham." Inclining his head, Nathaniel smiled at them both, the package in his pocket suddenly beginning to burn through his clothes, making him wonder if Lady Smithton ought to know about his intentions towards Miss Bavidge.

"Good afternoon," Lady Smithton replied. "How do you fare this afternoon?"

"Very well, indeed!" Nathaniel answered, feeling a happiness bubble up within him that had not been present for some time. "I am very much looking forward to the ball this evening, I must say."

"As am I," Lord Havisham interjected, which made Lady Smithton smile. "It should be a most excellent evening."

Nathaniel was about to say more when a foreboding presence drew near to Lady Smithton. His smile faded to black almost at once, his brows drawing close together as Lady Smithton turned her head to see who had caught Nathaniel's attention.

"How good to see you again, Morton!" Lord Rochester's voice was filled with glee—an expression which Nathaniel did not like in the least. "I have, in the last half hour, enjoyed the company of Miss Bavidge! How glad I am to know that she is not at all committed to you alone."

Nathaniel felt his heart quicken, felt a flush begin to creep up his cheeks, but remained as outwardly calm and as collected as he could. "Good afternoon, Lord Rochester," he replied, gesturing towards Lady Smithton and Lord Havisham, who were both standing together with identical looks of dislike on their faces. "Lord Havisham, Lady Smithton, and I were just conversing, as you can see, so if you please—"

His attempt at trying to remove Lord Rochester's presence from them failed entirely, for Lord Rochester only lifted one eyebrow and gave Lord Havisham and Lady Smithton a cursory glance only. This brought anger to Lord Havisham's expression, whereas Lady Smithton merely lifted her chin and held Lord Rochester's gaze steadily, proving to them all that she was not about to be intimidated by this rude gentleman and his ignorant manner.

"As I said," Lord Rochester continued, grinning darkly at Lady Smithton before returning his attention to Nathaniel. "I have been enjoying the company of Miss Bavidge very recently, indeed. It was good to walk with her and speak to her of a good many things."

Nathaniel's anger immediately faded as a cold hand gripped his heart. Lord Rochester had spoken to Miss Bavidge? What was it precisely he had said?

"And she has, of course, accepted my request to court her also," Lord Rochester continued airily. "I do not think your courtship will continue on in the same fashion, Lord Morton, for she has made herself quite clear in this matter." He chuckled, the sound seeming to darken the bright summer's day. "What a shame you shall not be able to call her your own for much longer."

"In this, I know you are quite mistaken, Lord Rochester," Lady Smithton spoke up, her expression taut as she looked directly into Lord Rochester's face, her hands reaching to rest on her hips. "Miss Bavidge has nothing but contempt for you. No, you need not protest." She shook her head and held up one hand to silence Lord Rochester's attempts to convince her otherwise. "I have heard from her lips those exact words, sir. She was fully aware of the kind of gentleman you are, given that she stumbled upon you attempting to take advantage of a young lady whose will you had so easily bent." Lady Smithton's voice became a little brittle, her words hitting Lord Rochester like sharp stones. "So I have no doubt, Lord Rochester, that you are telling nothing but untruths in the hope of spreading confusion and doubt." She threw a quick glance towards Nathaniel, trying to encourage him that they, at the very least, did not trust Lord Rochester. "I do not think we have anything more to say, Lord Rochester. If you will excuse us." She did not move but remained precisely where she was, spreading out one hand towards the pavement to her left as an obvious and decisive gesture.

Lord Rochester, however, did not take even a single step in the direction Lady Smithton suggested. He looked back at Lady Smithton for some moments, not saying a single word but holding Lady Smithton's gaze. Nathaniel thought it was his way of attempting to frighten her, to intimidate her somewhat, but the gentleman clearly did not know Lady Smithton particularly well if he thought she would quail before him.

"I believe Lady Smithton has asked you to depart from her side, Lord Rochester." This time it was Lord Havisham who spoke, his voice low and threatening. "Might I suggest that you do as she wishes."

Lord Rochester made to say something only to stop himself. Turning his gaze back to Nathaniel, he chuckled softly, the sound seeming so out of place in what was an otherwise discomfiting situation.

"You do not believe me," he murmured, shrugging. "That is quite understandable. You shall see for yourselves this evening, then. I am quite certain that I will be proven right. Your courtship will come to an end, Lord Morton, and there I shall be, ready to scoop up Miss Bavidge in your place. Although my intentions for her are certainly not as pure as yours might be." He laughed aloud at this, making Nathaniel's hands curl into fist as he glared at the gentleman, wishing that he could plant the man a facer right in the middle of the London street.

"Thankfully, I can trust that Miss Bavidge had a good deal more sense than to do something so foolish," Nathaniel retorted, removing the smile from Lord Rochester's face, his eyes darkening. "Even if she does wish to end our courtship, I can be certain in my belief that she will not go into your arms. Lady Smithton knows that as well as I, Lord Rochester. Your lies shall do no good here." He gestured to the pavement, just as Lady Smithton had done. "Nor is your company welcome any longer."

Lord Rochester's lip curled angrily, his eyes now holding a good deal of fury. "Why do you not ask Lord Morton what it is he has been hiding?" he asked, turning his head towards Lady Smithton as he began to walk away. "Ask him why he has always had such an interest in Miss Bavidge." He slapped Nathaniel hard on the shoulder as he passed, making Nathaniel twist away from him. "Tell them, Morton. Tell them why you have sought Miss Bavidge out from the very first moment you arrived in town. Tell them why you felt such guilt over her. Tell them what it is you have been keeping hidden from them all for so long. And have no fear," he chuckled again, and Nathaniel's stomach twisted. "I have already spoken to Miss Bavidge about it all, so your confession to her is not required. Although the consequences of it have already taken hold. Good day!"

Nathaniel closed his eyes tightly, hating that Lord Rochester had spoken in such a manner but feeling the weight of his responsibility begin to fall on him once more. There came a few moments of silence, and even though Nathaniel had his eyes shut, he could feel the confused gaze of Lady Smithton resting on him.

"Lord Morton?" Lady Smithton asked, eventually, forcing Nathaniel to open his eyes and give her his attention. "Just what, might I ask, is Lord Rochester speaking of?"

Nathaniel let out a long, slow breath, feeling his stomach still twisting this way and that. "I have not yet informed Miss Bavidge of this, Lady Smithton," he said, seeing how Lord Havisham also looked concerned. "I have had every intention of doing so, but as yet, I have been unable to speak to her of it. And as each day has passed, as I have felt my affection rise up within my heart, my fear of speaking the truth to her has grown."

Lady Smithton frowned, although she did not appear angry. "Just what is it you have yet to speak to her about?" she asked quietly. "If I might be so bold as to ask."

Nathaniel swallowed hard, ran one hand across his forehead, and then resettled his hat. The time had come to speak the truth. "I discovered what Lord Hawkridge was intending," he said, seeing Lady Smithton's eyes widen. "Instead of keeping it to myself, I went directly to the Earl of Knighton—the gentleman he was intending to blackmail—and spoke to him of it all. I believe it was this that put an end to Lord Hawkridge's intentions."

Lady Smithton said nothing for some moments, although her eyes were bright with both surprise and dismay. Lord Havisham cleared his throat gruffly, looking to Lady Smithton and then to Nathaniel himself.

"I did not know of this," Lord Havisham muttered as though he were apologizing to Lady Smithton for some reason. "I was entirely unaware of it."

"That does not matter for the moment," came Lady Smithton's gentle reply, her eyes still on Nathaniel. "Might I ask, Lord Morton, whether your interest in Miss Bavidge came from a sense of guilt over what you had done?"

"I knew I had done right," Nathaniel replied quickly. "However, the truth is, Lady Smithton, I did something entirely foolish. Feeling the weight of it on my mind, I spoke to my friend about what I had discovered. This friend did not keep it to himself, as he had said he would, and, thus, the word was spread all through London." Biting his lip, Nathaniel sighed heavily, feeling a heavy weight on his shoulders. "Knowing what would be waiting for Miss Bavidge should she return to society, I endeavored to attempt, in some way, to aid her in her return."

"And in doing so, found yourself quite in love with her," Lady Smithton finished, with such a certainty in her voice that Nathaniel looked at her sharply. "Oh yes," she continued, seeing his surprised look. "I am well aware that you have a great depth of feeling for Miss Bavidge. Also, I can understand why you have struggled to speak to her about what you have done, for it does, in a way, mean that you have some responsibility in her struggles within society."

"Believe me, I wanted very much to keep the affair to myself," Nathaniel said honestly, praying that Lady Smithton would believe him. "I tried to keep it as quiet as possible, aware of what the gossip mongers would do should they discover it. Speaking to Lord Rochester was quite foolish of me, however. I knew of his foibles and yet still believed that he would remain silent about the matter I had brought him. How wrong I was!"

Lord Havisham cleared his throat again, trying to re-enter the conversation. "And you have not spoken to Miss Bavidge of this, Lord Morton?" There was a slight accusatory tone to his voice, but Nathaniel accepted it without question.

"I have had every intention of doing so for some time," he admitted. "Although previously, I wanted merely to hide it from her. However, since I have discovered that my heart is involved with Miss Bavidge, I have struggled to know what to say and how to say it. And now, it seems, Lord Rochester has taken his truth and plunged it directly between myself and Miss Bavidge." He ran one hand over his face, a small groan escaping his lips. "And I do not know what it is she will think of me now."

Lady Smithton hesitated, then took a step closer to him, her expression softening. "It will have been a shock, yes," she admitted, honestly. "But I believe that Miss Bavidge has a good deal of affection for you also, Lord Morton. Trust that she will simply need a little time to consider what she has discovered. Speak to her. Tell her the truth again so that she may hear it from your lips. Apologize that you have not spoken to her of it before this day but tell her the truth about *why* you have hidden it from her. Tell her of your heart's affection. Miss Bavidge is reasonable and levelheaded. I know precisely what she thinks of Lord Rochester. I doubt that she will allow such things to overwhelm her and certainly will not believe them outright, not when it has been Lord Rochester to speak of them!" She shook her head lightly and then smiled up at him. "Have no fear, Lord Morton. I know that your heart is engaged to her own and in being aware of that, I must confess that I am able to understand your delay in speaking the truth to her. Not that I think it wise, but I must pray that it will not bring an end to an acquaintance that appears to have brought you both such happiness."

Nathaniel nodded, grateful that Lady Smithton had not rejected him outright and appeared, in fact, to be quite understanding. "That is most kind of you, Lady Smithton."

"Have hope, Lord Morton, that all will find its resolve," she told him, returning to Lord Havisham and putting one hand on his arm. "I shall speak to Miss Bavidge on your behalf if it is required, to talk through the matter further, but I must hope that it will not be necessary." With a small smile in Lord Havisham's direction, she attempted to brighten the mood. "If you will excuse us, Lord Morton. I have asked Lord Havisham his opinion of the gowns that some of my *dear* girls are to wear to the next few occasions. And that will, I fear, take a good few hours."

Nathaniel shot a look towards Lord Havisham, who seemed visibly deflated. It was quite clear to Nathaniel that the gentleman was not at all inclined towards doing as Lady Smithton asked but was doing so precisely because it was she who had asked it.

"But of course."

Such a tumult of emotions and fears settled in Nathaniel's stomach as he again thanked Lady Smithton and took his leave of both her and Lord Havisham. Lord Havisham had said very little but was clearly thinking through a great deal, his jaw set and his expression a little irritated. Was he angry that he had not been able to discover this prior to Lord Rochester's meeting with them on the busy London street?

Sighing heavily, Nathaniel turned his face back towards his carriage and hurried towards it, no longer feeling as joyful nor as content as he had only half an hour before. He could not ask Miss Bavidge to marry him this evening now, could he? Not when he was aware that Lord Rochester had done all he could to disrupt Nathaniel's acquaintance with Miss Bavidge. Perhaps he ought to ensure that Miss Bavidge understood everything and, thereafter, give her as much time as was required for her to consider everything and, hopefully, forgive him for his delay before he considered asking her to be his wife. Or, alternatively, he ought to do precisely as he had planned, to prove to her the depth of his affections.

Groaning aloud, Nathaniel climbed into his carriage and, sitting down, threw his head back in frustration. He had delayed too long in speaking to Miss Bavidge, believing himself to be safe from Lord Rochester given that Miss Bavidge herself made it quite clear she now avoided the gentleman completely, but in delaying he had only made matters a good deal worse. He could not imagine what Miss Bavidge had felt as Lord Rochester had told her what Nathaniel himself ought to have done. Had she been greatly upset? Confused? Mayhap she had simply laughed off Lord Rochester's comments and did not, as yet, believe them to be true. One thing he could be certain of: Lord Rochester had no hold over Miss Bavidge's heart. She was too wise, too sensible to allow herself to be drawn in. He would remain unable to fulfill his intentions towards the lady and that, in its own way, brought a good deal of relief.

All he could do now was pray that she would not turn

away from him completely, that she would give him the time to explain all that he had done and his reasons behind it. That she would listen as he spoke to her from his heart and of the love that had begun to grow within, and that perhaps, with a little luck, she would respond in the very same way.

CHAPTER FOURTEEN

"Good evening, Lord Morton."

Nathaniel greeted his host at once, bowing quickly. "Good evening, Lord Knighton. Might I say that this evening looks to be quite spectacular! A remarkable occasion, to be sure." He smiled at Lady Knighton, who blushed at his compliment. "You have quite excelled yourself, Lady Knighton."

Lord Knighton drew in his breath in mock horror. "You mean to say that you believe I have had nothing whatsoever to do with this occasion?" he asked as his wife blushed all the more. "You think me lazy and uninspiring?"

Nathaniel chuckled. "No, not at all. It is only that I believe that your wife has a good deal more creativity in such matters, Lord Knighton."

His host chuckled and threw a long look towards his wife, who caught his eye and smiled back at him. "In that, you are quite correct, Lord Morton," he agreed, chuckling. "Of course, all the thanks should go to my dear lady, who has put her heart and soul into this occasion." He gestured to the ball itself, where dancers had already taken to the floor. "It is quite magnificent, my dear. You have, as Lord Morton says, excelled yourself."

"Thank you," Lady Knighton replied, demurely. "You are *both* very kind."

Nathaniel smiled and inclined his head. "Might I also thank you for your willingness to invite Miss Bavidge and her aunt," he said, seeing the look of contentedness fade slightly from both Lord and Lady Knighton's faces. "I am aware of the rumors that have gone on about both yourself and her father, Lord Knighton, and also understand that there may be some gossip spread about this evening and her presence here, but I am truly grateful that you have been willing to invite her nonetheless."

Lord Knighton hesitated, cleared his throat, and then shrugged. "I will not pretend that it was a simple matter, Lord Morton, but my conscience was pricked by your request and my own dear wife's encouragement to do what I knew to be correct. Miss Bavidge is not her father. She was not caught up in his scheme in any way. Therefore, I know full well that she has every right to be present amongst society and to continue without any rebuttal from anyone."

"That is easier to do than to say, I know," Nathaniel said quickly. "It would be quite understandable if you wished to disassociate yourself from Miss Bavidge, but I am very glad that you have such a kind heart, Lord Knighton."

"And you also," Lady Knighton added with a quick smile. "You also have a kind heart, Lord Morton, for you have sought that lady out and done what you can to bring her back into society's fold, pushing aside the whispers and rumors with barely more than an acknowledgment." Her knowing smile told Nathaniel that Lady Knighton was fully aware of all that had gone on between himself and Miss Bavidge of late, making him shift a trifle uncomfortably. "I do wonder if, Lord Morton, your intentions for Miss Bavidge herself are no longer a simple desire to see her accepted by the *beau monde*."

Nathaniel made to answer, stammering horribly, only for Lord Knighton to laugh and wave a hand, breaking off Nathaniel's reply.

"My wife is always so observant," he chuckled, as Nathaniel let out a breath of relief. "But I shall not force you to stand here and answer. I am sure that you wish to go to join the other guests, particularly given that Miss Bavidge herself is already arrived." He wiggled his brows and chuckled, making Nathaniel let out a bark of laughter that took some of his nervousness away.

"She is arrived, you say?" he asked, taking a small step away from his host and looking out towards the crowd. "When?"

"Only a few minutes before you," Lord Knighton replied, with a grin. "I am certain you shall find her very quickly, Lord Morton. A gentleman does not like to be kept from his prize."

Nathaniel gave Lord Knighton a wry grin, thanked them both again, and took his leave, suddenly determined to find Miss Bavidge and speak to her just as soon as he was able. The weight on his mind would not fade until he had done just that, which meant he had to discover her just as soon as he could.

It took some minutes of walking through the crowd and turning this way and that before he finally caught sight of Miss Bavidge. She was wearing a gown of light blue, her hair piled up on the back of her head. However, she was not looking towards him but when she turned her head and saw him, she looked down to the floor almost at once. She turned her head a little further away from him, and a knot formed in Nathaniel's stomach at her actions.

And then, his gaze fell on Lord Rochester. He was standing by Miss Bavidge's side, speaking to her in what appeared to be a most intimate fashion. Anger flared in Nathaniel's heart, and he hurried towards them both, wondering what it was that Lord Rochester was saying to Miss Bavidge on this occasion, only for Lord Rochester's gaze to fall upon him. A broad grin spread across Rochester's face, making Nathaniel's anger burn hot with a furious fire as his steps quickened, determined to reach both Lord Rochester and Miss Bavidge without delay.

Lord Rochester leaned forward, said something in Miss Bavidge's ear, and, much to Nathaniel's surprise, Miss Bavidge nodded and then turned away. Lord Rochester remained beside her, leading her towards the open doors that led to Lord Knighton's gardens, whilst another young lady trailed after them, her expression deeply uncertain.

Nathaniel froze in place, not quite certain what to do next. He could not believe what he had just witnessed, for he had never once thought that Miss Bavidge would go anywhere willingly with Lord Rochester. Why had she gone out to the gardens with him? It could not be that she had decided to accept Lord Rochester's attentions, surely? She was much too intelligent and wise to do something so foolish.

His feet felt like thick wooden logs that weighed him down as he tried to make his way towards the doors. His breath was catching in his chest, his throat rasping and his mouth burning with a fierce and furious heat, making him feel as though he might explode with both fury and confusion at any given moment. Stumbling outside, he held onto the rail that led him down three small steps, wondering where Miss Bavidge and Lord Rochester might have gone.

At least she is accompanied, he told himself, seeing the darkness of the evening begin to swallow up the guests who walked out of doors. *But why has she gone with him?*

Stumbling badly, Nathaniel moved as fast as he could, feeling his heart clamor wildly within his chest. He had to find her. He had to prevent Lord Rochester from saying anything more, had to encourage her not to listen nor believe the lies that he was certain would come from Lord Rochester's mouth. The stones on the path crunched under his feet as he walked swiftly forward, his hands curling into fists as he centered his attention on finding Miss Bavidge.

A small cry caught his ears, making him stop dead. Turning slowly, he looked all about him, trying to discover where the sound might have come from, but nothing came into view. Another sound made his heart come to a sudden stop, skipping a beat as fear clutched at his soul. Where was Miss Bavidge?

Hardly daring to breathe but knowing that he could not remain standing so quietly and silently, Nathaniel took a deep breath and turned to his left, coming off the path and walking onto the grass. The gardens were large for a London townhouse and had plenty of small spaces where one might hide—although he could not even begin to think that Miss Bavidge had gone willingly from the path with Lord Rochester.

Another sound, one he could not quite make out, came to him and Nathaniel hurried forward a little more, his eyes searching every part of the gardens he could see.

And then, he saw her.

She was in Lord Rochester's arms, being held tightly, whilst the other young lady who had been accompanying them stood, shocked and confused, a few steps away. Nathaniel could barely breathe, seeing Lord Rochester lift his head and, in doing so, catching Nathaniel's eye. A slow smile spread across his face, sending a wave of nausea into Nathaniel's stomach. This could not be. This could not be occurring, not when he had believed Miss Bavidge to be so wise. She could not possibly have gone to Lord Rochester, not when she had kissed Nathaniel only a couple of days ago! Her words had been filled with promise, filled with hope, but now as he looked at her, seeing her twist out of Lord Rochester's embrace, the light in his heart began to dim.

Miss Bavidge saw him, her eyes flaring, and her hand pressed against her chest. "Lord Morton," she whispered, taking a few steps towards him, although she walked unsteadily, clearly overcome by the heat of Lord Rochester's attentions. "Lord Morton, I—"

"Have you not something to ask Lord Morton?" Lord Rochester hurried forward, grasping Miss Bavidge's arm with one hand and gesturing towards Nathaniel. "Have you not to ask him whether what I have said is true?"

Miss Bavidge did not seem to be completely in charge of her senses, for she blinked rapidly, then looked up at Lord Rochester before dropping her gaze to where his hand had settled on her arm. She closed her eyes tightly and pulled her arm away, obviously embarrassed that Nathaniel had seen such a thing.

"You knew my father." Her whisper was quiet, yet it seemed to fill the gardens, burning a fire of guilt in his heart.

"Yes, I did," he replied, honestly, trying not to feel the way his heart was slowly being pulled apart. "It is as Lord Rochester says. I discovered what he was doing and spoke to the Earl of Knighton about his intentions." He gave a small shrug, trying to ignore how Lord Rochester was grinning. "That is all. I was afraid to tell you for fear of what you would either say or do, Miss Bavidge."

Miss Bavidge swallowed hard, her eyes glistening with sudden tears.

"The more time we spent with each other, the more I realized that I did not want you to turn from me," Nathaniel finished helplessly. "How could I tell you what I had done? Could I hope that you would understand?"

Miss Bavidge shook her head, a tear streaking down her face. "I would never even have given you my name had I known what it was you did to both my father and to myself," she replied, her voice shaking with suppressed emotion. "I did not know the truth. You drew near to me with falsehood in your heart."

Nathaniel swallowed the sudden ache in his throat, seeing her anger and upset and praying that she would let those emotions flood away so that she would consider what else lay in her heart—only to recall what he had seen of her and Lord Rochester. His heart dropped to the ground, shattering into pieces. She had clearly already set herself against him. She had gone to Lord Rochester, just as Rochester himself had predicated.

"Rochester will use you for his own ends," he rasped, slicing the air with his hand in a sudden fit of anger. "You have believed every word he has said without even considering that it might be false. You have—"

"You have just admitted that he speaks the truth!" Miss Bavidge protested, her voice louder now with an evident anger in her words. "You have just admitted that you spoke to Lord Knighton of my father, and thereafter, the news was spread about all of London."

Nathaniel lifted his chin, aware that this was one of the saddest moments that he had experienced thus far, but also that he was not about to allow her to spread guilt over him for a choice had made. A choice that, whilst difficult for her to accept mayhap, one that had been made in the right spirit and with the correct desire—the desire that an innocent gentleman not be taken advantage of by some misguided individual who wanted nothing other than to take some of the gentleman's wealth as his own.

"I shall not apologize, Miss Bavidge, for what I have done. Rather, I intend to stand by it, to state unequivocally that, should I be faced with such a decision again, I would do the very same." He saw Miss Bavidge take a small step back as if he had slapped her, but he steadied his resolve regardless. "I may have been foolish in what I chose to do thereafter, but I shall never regret preventing Lord Knighton from being so treated." Seeing how she dropped her head, Nathaniel felt his heart twist in his chest, both shocked and horrified at how she had seemingly returned to Lord Rochester without any consideration. Their courtship, it seemed, was over, just as Lord Rochester had stated it would be. Quite how he had engineered it, Nathaniel was not certain, but there had been no mistaking what he had seen. The desire to turn away, to look anywhere but Miss Bavidge's face, grew forcefully within him until he could not help but give in.

"I shall leave you to your... companion," he said, harshly, throwing the words over his shoulder as he retreated towards the path. "Goodbye, Miss Bavidge."

If she responded, Nathaniel did not hear her. His heart ached far too much, his head swimming with confusing and conflicting thoughts that seemed to bore into his mind. Pain etched itself over his forehead, spreading across his skull as he made his way back inside, no longer finding even the smallest enjoyment in the gathering nor the music within.

"Lord Morton!"

He could barely focus, only just managing to lift his head to see Lady Smithton come into view.

"Lord Morton, whatever has occurred?" Lady

Smithton asked, sounding quite horrified. "You look quite done in."

Nathaniel found his mouth was much too heavy to form words, his chest rising and falling with each breath he took. He saw Lady Smithton's look of alarm grow even bigger as he shook his head wordlessly, felt her hand press upon his arm.

"You must not leave," she said, firmly, looking directly up into his face. "You must not. Whatever has occurred, we must resolve it."

Nathaniel lowered his head, his eyes squeezing shut so as to close out the sight of Lady Smithton, to hide himself away from lights and sounds of the ball going on all around him. The memory of Miss Bavidge in Lord Rochester's arms threw itself back into his mind, making a groan escape from his mouth. This, in turn, made Lady Smithton's hand tighten on his arm, her fear now evident in her face as he opened his eyes to look at her.

"Lord Rochester," he rasped, hearing how decrepit his voice sounded. "He..." Trailing off, he gestured behind him just as someone knocked into him, hard, pushing him forward. Stumbling, he caught himself just in time, regaining his balance and turning around to see none other than the young lady who had been escorting Miss Bavidge grasping desperately onto Lady Smithton's arm, gesturing wildly with the other hand and tugging Lady Smithton forward. Lady Smithton went white, her eyes suddenly blazing with apparent anger, and she hurried forward without another word to Nathaniel. Lord Havisham, having just appeared behind Lady

Smithton, followed them also, evidently aware that something was not at all right.

Blinking, Nathaniel tried to regain some of his composure, looking all about him to see if he had garnered any attention. Thankfully, it seemed that the majority of the *ton* were much too busy with their conversations and dances, meaning that none of them were particularly interested in anything that had just occurred.

Shaking his head as though to clear it, Nathaniel took in one long breath. Lady Smithton had asked him to remain, not to leave as he had first intended—but why should he do as she asked? What would be the reason to stay? Miss Bavidge had made herself clear and had ripped his heart from his body in wrapping her arms about Lord Rochester instead of about him, as he had dreamed of. Her sorrow and anger over his decision to speak to Lord Knighton about her father's intentions to blackmail him had taken him aback completely. He had thought she might understand why he had done such a thing, for he knew full well that she accepted her father's actions had been wrong. A part of him wanted to believe that she had spoken so out of hurt that he had not been honest with her, which he could well understand, but that had not been clear from her words. He had lost her forever, it seemed. She had turned away from him and had chosen to fall into Lord Rochester's arms instead. Perhaps he had never really known the truth of her character at all.

Nathaniel was in a state of shock. Thinking perhaps he should leave the ball entirely, Nathaniel began to weave his way aimlessly through the crowd of guests, their laughter and smiles beating down upon his already heavy shoulders. He felt as though he could no longer be one of them, that any modicum of happiness had been ripped from him completely. There was nothing left here for him now. The rest of the season would be dull and lonely, wafting nothing but sadness and sorrow over his heart. There was no use in staying in London, he reasoned. Mayhap, even the morrow, he might begin to make arrangements to return to his estate.

You must not leave. Whatever has occurred, we must resolve it.

Lady Smithton's words began to wind their way through Nathaniel's morose mind, reminding him of how Lady Smithton had appeared when the second young lady, whose name he knew but could not recollect, had come charging into the ballroom to search for her. A slight twinge of unease buried itself into his heart, making him hesitate as he placed one foot in front of the other, more or less making his way to the door.

Something was clearly wrong. Most likely, it was simply that the young lady had been as shocked as he over Miss Bavidge's and Lord Rochester's behavior and not known what else to do other than seek out Lady Smithton. Mayhap, in her fright, she had stood stock still for a few minutes, frozen in place, until she had regained her senses and gone in search of the lady. Most likely, Lady Smithton was doing all she could to smooth matters, or otherwise, she was insisting that the two announce their engagement at once. Another painful bite tore into his heart. Would Miss Bavidge end up becoming Lord Rochester's bride? He could think of nothing worse, for Miss Bavidge was not at all suited to such a dark character as Rochester—but what was he to do about it?

What if there is something wrong?

The question made him stop dead, his heart thundering furiously as he considered matters. If there was even the smallest chance that there was something wrong, that he had made even the tiniest error in judgment, then did he not owe it to both himself and to Miss Bavidge to discover what the truth was? Could he really return home, return to his estate, without discovering why the young lady had been so frantic in her desire to have Lady Smithton hurry out to the gardens? He might assume that it was simply to do with Miss Bavidge and Lord Rochester's improper behavior, but there was a chance that he was wrong.

Groaning aloud at his indecision and at weakness when it came to Miss Bavidge, Nathaniel forced himself to turn back around and walk towards the doors to the gardens once more. Each step felt heavier than the last, his regret growing ever stronger. Certain that he would come upon a sight that would only add to his pain all the more, Nathaniel gritted his teeth and forced himself outside. The three short steps led him back to the path where he had been only a few minutes before, although he could see no sign of anyone.

And then, a shout rippled around the gardens, although it was soon swallowed up by the sound of music and laughter that ran from the open doors. There were only a few others out walking outside and none of them, Nathaniel noticed, seemed to pay any attention to the sound. His ears strained to hear more, but nothing came.

Forcing himself to walk from the path to the grass, just as he had done before, Nathaniel made his way carefully forward, underneath the branches of a tree and feeling himself encased in shadow a little more. The light was fading fast, and it was difficult to make anything out.

"How dare you?"

A male voice scurried towards him, although the words were not directed towards himself. Frowning, Nathaniel moved forward as silently as he could, only to see a gentleman he did not recognize planting a facer upon another. The second fell back with a small cry, stumbling back and hitting his head on a tree trunk. Much to Nathaniel's horror, the man collapsed to the ground, which garnered a gasp from three others whom he had not, as yet, noticed. They appeared to be three ladies, which he immediately presumed to be Lady Smithton, Miss Bavidge, and the other young lady whose name he could not recall. Confusion tore through his mind as he returned his gaze to the gentleman still standing, seeing him move forward to the fallen one and bend down for a moment.

"He lives still," he said, gruffly, making Nathaniel realize that it was none other than Lord Havisham who spoke. "Knocked out cold for the time being."

"Mayhap that is for the best," came the soft voice of Lady Smithton. "We must decide what we are to do now. This cannot be allowed to continue." Her head turned towards Nathaniel, although he felt sure she could not see him in the shadow of the tree.

He was about to be proven wrong.

"You may as well come out and join us, Lord

Morton." Lady Smithton's voice was clear yet firm, bringing a sudden flush of embarrassment to Nathaniel as he stepped out and made his way slowly towards the group. "Can I say that I am very glad you have not left us as I feared you might?" She gestured towards Miss Bavidge, who had her head bowed low. "I think there is a good deal of misunderstanding and it is vastly important that the truth is made known, for both your sakes." She smiled at him encouragingly, although even in the gloom, Nathaniel did not miss the hard glint in her eye. "Shall we sit here?" She gestured to two benches that sat at a right angle with a small glowing lantern between them. "Lord Havisham, if you would—"

"I shall not leave the scoundrel for a moment," Lord Havisham grated, his threat more than apparent. "You need have no doubt about that."

Nathaniel blinked. "Scoundrel?" he repeated, not understanding why Lord Rochester would be referred to in such a way when surely Miss Bavidge had gone into his arms willingly.

"As I have said," Lady Smithton replied quickly. "There is a good deal to set right. Please, do sit, Lord Morton, so that we might begin."

Having no other option and barely able to look towards Miss Bavidge, who still had her head bowed low, Nathaniel chose to do as Lady Smithton asked and, without a word, followed her to the benches.

CHAPTER FIFTEEN

*E*mma knew she had been foolish.

Her hurt and pain over what Lord Rochester had said had not left her all through her preparations for the evening's ball. Her confusion about the truth of it all had swirled about her like a fog, and she had not had the opportunity to speak of it to anyone. Her aunt, as usual, had no consideration for her and had barely said a word when they had made their way to the ball. Sitting in the carriage, Emma had felt tears burning in her eyes but had refused to let even a single one fall, steeling herself against them so that her aunt would have no reason to question her in any way. Not that she would have expressed any true concern for Emma, of course. It would merely have been the urge to prevent Emma from garnering any more attention from the *beau monde* so that her aunt would not have any further difficulties.

Entering the ballroom, Emma had been almost immediately found by Miss Crosby, who had linked arms with her and drawn her further into the room. Emma had not been particularly talkative, however, making Miss Crosby express concern for her, but Emma had chosen not to reveal a single thing. Instead, she had determined silently that she would either find Lord Rochester or Lord Morton and demand the truth from them.

How unfortunate it had been that Lord Rochester had been the one she had found first—although part of her now suspected that he had been waiting for her. Emma had tried to speak boldly, to let him understand in no uncertain terms that she needed to know that what he had said to her earlier about Lord Morton's involvement with her father and the gossip that had come thereafter had all been entirely true, but Lord Rochester had simply laughed and left her floundering.

He had leaned over her, intimidating her as best he could, and stated that if she did not believe him, then all she had to do was seek out Lord Morton and ask it of him. The truth would come from his lips and would confirm every word Lord Rochester had said.

Emma had not wanted to believe it. Miss Crosby had been frowning heavily in Lord Rochester's direction, making her dislike for him and her concern for Emma more than apparent, but Emma had not known what to do. To find Lord Morton and to ask him outright what he had done seemed horrifying, for if he admitted it to be true, then that left her with nothing. She would have to do so, she realized, feeling as though her dreams and hopes were beginning to crack all about her, threatening to shatter at any moment. Her head had hung low, her heart aching furiously with a terrible pain. The heat of the room had burned in her cheeks, and a trickle of sweat had run down her spine. Lord Rochester had leaned over her again, stating that mayhap she might like to take a turn out of doors, through the doors to her left.

Why she had agreed, Emma did not know. She had been foolish enough to do so without thinking, her heart still filled with Lord Morton, but her mind filled with questions over his conduct and whether she could state that she knew him at all.

The next few minutes had been nothing but a blur. With Miss Crosby behind her, she had let out a small cry when Lord Rochester had grasped her arm and tugged her from the path and onto the grass, chuckling loudly as he did so. Emma had not known what to do, struggling against him with a fear crashing over her. When he had hauled her into his arms, she had tried to push him away, her hands resting on his shoulders as he attempted to kiss her again. Even now, as she thought of it, a cold sweat broke out across her brow. Lord Rochester had been so strong and determined that had it not been for Miss Crosby's exclamation of both shock and fright that had distracted Lord Rochester, then she might never have been able to tug herself out of his arms.

Except, she had done so only to see Lord Morton standing near to Miss Crosby, his face white and eyes wide. Her heart had been tugged from her chest by the pain in his expression, her body heaving with ragged breaths as she attempted to find some sort of composure.

Except Lord Morton had done nothing more than add to her torment. Barely able to look at him as he sat on the other bench alone, Emma closed her eyes tightly against the flood of tears that burned. In her shock, in her horror that Lord Morton had seen what she had been doing, she had found a flurry of questions flying from her mouth as though to cover what he had seen of her, and Lord Morton had failed her with almost every answer.

He had stood by his decision to ruin her reputation by gossiping about her father's attempt at blackmail. She had no upset over his intention to *prevent* the blackmail from taking place, but the fact that he had admitted to speaking of it to others without hindrance had torn at her. How could he have done such a thing when he knew precisely what it would do to her? Was it because of guilt that he had sought her out at the start of this season? Was his supposed affection for her true? Or was it simply that he felt such guilt over what he had done that he had no other choice but to attempt to court her?

"Now," Lady Smithton began, softly. "I must begin by stating to Miss Crosby that you, my dear girl, have done nothing untoward." She reached across and patted Miss Crosby's hand, who immediately burst into tears. "It would not be the first time that a young lady has found herself frozen in place by both shock and fright. I quite understand what happened. You must not blame yourself."

Despite her pain, Emma saw the sorrow and upset in Miss Crosby's eyes and, reaching across, squeezed her hand with her own. Miss Crosby had been so shocked by Lord Rochester's behavior that she had stared, stunned, at what had been occurring without being able to move. It had only been when Lord Morton had retreated and Lord Rochester had begun to advance towards Emma again that Miss Crosby had found the strength in her limbs and had been forced to leave Emma to retreat from Lord Rochester in any way she could so that she might seek out further aid. Emma was more than grateful for her efforts, for to bring both Lady Smithton and Lord Havisham had ensured that Lord Rochester had not been able to succeed in his attempts. She had been busy trying to find a way back towards the path and back to the ball, whilst Lord Rochester had been determined to keep her far from them as possible, advancing slowly and pushing her further back into the gardens.

Wiping at her forehead with a trembling hand, Emma closed her eyes tightly and let out a long, slow breath. The ordeal was over, although a good deal of pain still remained.

"Lord Morton," Lady Smithton continued, calmly. "You and Miss Bavidge will need to speak at length, I believe. To that end, myself and Miss Crosby shall go to Lord Havisham and come up with some idea as to what we ought to do with that blaggard." Her expression grew dark, but her chin lifted. "Might I suggest that what you believe of Miss Bavidge to be entirely incorrect. And Miss Bavidge." She turned her head to look at Emma directly. "You must also be certain that everything Lord Rochester told you cannot be trusted. I believe that he has deliberately misled you in some matter or other, but in a most twisted fashion so as to set you both asunder." She shrugged and got to her feet. "Purely for his own pleasure, of course," she finished, as Miss Crosby also rose. "That sort of man is no gentleman." Without another word, she linked arms with Miss Crosby and led her carefully towards Lord Havisham, murmuring encouraging words.

Emma could barely look at Lord Morton. Her eyes drifted towards him but could not quite meet his gaze, for her cheeks flushed hot, and her heart began to beat with such an agonized yearning that it was all she could do to contain her tears.

"Are you quite all right, Miss Bavidge?"

Lord Morton's voice was soft, although she could still see, in the dim light, that his expression was troubled.

"I am not," she replied, her voice tremulous. "This evening has been.... truly terrible."

Lord Morton let out a long breath, leaned forward, and raked his hand through his hair. "I am to believe, then, given what Lady Smithton has said, that you were not doing as I first thought when I came upon you." He looked up at her, a faint hope burning in his eyes.

"No," Emma replied, steadying herself and curling her fingers around the arm of the bench. "No, I was not, Lord Morton. Lord Rochester—he..." She could not bring herself to form the words, shaking her head instead. "I was foolish to go out of doors with him, of course. I do not pretend otherwise."

Lord Morton let out a long breath, passing a hand over his eyes and groaning aloud. "My dear Miss Bavidge, I am truly sorry."

"Sorry?" She looked at him, not understanding.

"I am truly sorry that I believed you to be willingly going into Lord Rochester's arms," he replied, his voice hoarse with evident grief and regret. "Now that I think of it, now that I go back in my mind to what I saw, I realize now that you were being held in Lord Rochester's arms against your will. The horror that had fixed Miss Crosby to the ground, the sounds that I had heard..." He winced hard and buried his head in his hands. "Oh, Miss Bavidge. I can only apologize."

Her heart squeezed with both relief and pain. "Thank you, Lord Morton," she murmured, wondering how he could speak to her in such a gentle tone when she believed him to have already brought her a good deal of sorrow and struggle in spreading gossip about her father.

"Might I be so bold as to ask you why you left the ball with him?"

Emma closed her eyes, hating that she had been so foolish. "Because I was confused and upset," she stated, trying to keep her voice steady. "He told me many things about you, and as much as I did not want to believe them, I found my mind beginning to think that they were true."

Lord Morton let out another soft sigh, leaning forward so that his elbows rested on his knees and his hands linked together in front of him. "But they are true," he said, quietly, making her heart tear with pain. "I *did* speak to Lord Knighton about what I had discovered. I overheard your father boasting to some companion or other that he had found a young widow who was willing to state, quite brazenly, that she had a child by Lord Knighton but that he was refusing to acknowledge it." He swallowed hard, looking away from her. "He had promised her a good deal of wealth in return, of course. In discovering this, I knew precisely what I had to do. I had to tell Lord Knighton of it."

Emma knew that this had been the correct thing for

him to do, but still, the agony of being reminded what her father had done hit her like a thousand needles being pressed into her skin all at once. "Lord Knighton, I know, found the young lady in question and the matter was brought to a swift end," she replied, forcing herself to look into his face. "But I do not understand why you had to then gossip about what you had discovered to everyone you knew. Did you not once think about the consequences of such an action on myself? Was that why you sought me out, Lord Morton? So that your guilt might be assuaged?"

Her words rang through the garden, but for some moments, Lord Morton did not answer. Instead, he simply looked at her, his mouth a little ajar and his eyes wide. Emma did not know what to do, looking back at him and finding that he was clearly confused about what she had said. A sliver of doubt entered her mind. Had they, somehow, become mixed up in what had been said?

"Miss Bavidge...Emma." Lord Morton cleared his throat and swallowed hard before he continued, his hands tightening together. "I have never shared gossip about your father with anyone. I spoke to one gentleman of what had occurred in the belief that he would keep it entirely to himself." He spread his hands. "Do you not recall that I spoke to you of this very thing?"

Her throat tightened. "No," she replied, horrified to think that she had forgotten something so important. "No, I do not recall."

Lord Morton moved suddenly, catching her by surprise. He rose from his seat and came to sit down right beside her, immediately taking her hand in his. A great swell of emotion at his touch crested within her, sending tears to her eyes and a sob catching in her throat.

"My dear Emma, I believe we have both been dreadfully mistaken in one way or the next," Lord Morton said softly, looking deeply into her eyes. "I confess to you now that I have not told you the truth and that I should have done so from the very beginning. I should have told you that I was the one who discovered what your father intended to do and, thereafter, spoke to Lord Knightly of it so that the scheme could be ended."

Emma squeezed Lord Morton's fingers, feeling her heart slowly begin to knit back together. "I quite understand," she replied gently. "I would have much preferred that you would have told me the truth about my father and your part in it from the very beginning, however. Why did you not?"

Lord Morton lifted his other hand and settled it on top of their two joined ones. "Because I did not know how to bring the matter up," he replied, honestly. "I watched for you when you first arrived for the season, as I stated before. However, it was simply because of the guilt that I wished to eschew from my heart. The reason that the gossip and the rumors about your father and, in turn, yourself came about was because of my doing." Looking away, he let out a long, heavy breath and shook his head. "I told you that I spoke to Lord Rochester about something of grave importance, believing that he would remain silent about the matter." He looked back at her. "He did not. He told as many of the *beau monde* as he could about what he had learned from me. I confess, Miss Bavidge, that I was wrong to trust him, but at the time, he was my friend and I—foolishly or otherwise—believed what he promised."

"Then it was not your fault in any way," she said swiftly, not wanting him to feel any guilt that was not truly his to bear. "Nor shall I hear you suggest such a thing, Lord Morton."

"I felt it weighing on my mind," he told her, his fingers pressed over hers again. "I wanted to do all I could for you in whatever way I could so that your season would not be ruined by what had been a foolish misplacement of trust on my part." Another short pause. "But then I found myself quickly becoming enchanted with you, and I became afraid." She did not have time to ask him *what* he was afraid of, for he continued with his explanation. "Lord Rochester threatened to reveal all to you, as a consequence of my decision to end our friendship. If I warned you away from him, then he threatened to ensure that you knew everything."

Realization dawned. "And that is why you could not speak to me truthfully about Lord Rochester."

Lord Morton inclined his head, his eyes dropping to the ground at her feet. "I was a fool. I should have been honest with you from the start, Emma, but my heart and mind were so caught up with you and yet so deeply confused that I ended up floundering completely." He sighed but set his shoulders, lifting his head so that he could once more look deeply into her eyes. "I do not think I can bear to be without you, Emma," he said, his voice softening and his eyes gentle as he regarded her. "If you truly had turned away from me, then I do not think I would know what to do... aside from returning to my estate."

Emma blinked rapidly, seeing the genuine affection in his eyes and finding it almost impossible to breathe in a calm and unhurried fashion. "I should never have listened to Lord Rochester and allowed my mind such doubts, not when I know you to be a kind, amiable, and tender-hearted gentleman, Lord Morton," she replied, placing her free hand on top of his and seeing how he turned his hand so that he might interlace his fingers with her own. Her heart pounded furiously as she held his gaze, the evening's events and the darkness and pain that had swallowed her for some time finally beginning to fade away.

Lord Morton had made some mistakes and errors in judgment, but then again, so had she. The relief to know that it was not Lord Morton who had gossiped about her father's wrongdoing washed her pain and struggle away, leaving her only with a blissful hope and a developing contentedness. She could say nothing more, leaning closer to him and feeling the same feelings that she had experienced some days before beginning to burn within her.

This time, however, she did not have to press her face forward, for Lord Morton swept her up in an embrace that pulled her from her seat and forced her to fling her arms around his neck as he whirled her about. Laughing, Lord Morton set her down carefully and then kissed her fiercely, stealing her breath and throwing her senses into blissful confusion.

"I believe myself in love with you, Emma," he said

firmly, reaching down to capture her face with his gentle hands. "I believe myself to be *deeply* in love with you. I am not a man used to speaking of his emotions, but the truth will not let me alone until it is spoken." A small smile caught the corners of his mouth, making Emma smile back, her cheeks already flushed with color. Her anticipation building and not wanting to interrupt, she remained where she was, her hands around Lord Morton's neck and looking up into his face, waiting to see what he was to say.

"I love you, Emma," he said, with perhaps more firmness than she had expected. "Will you be my wife?"

There was no hesitation on her part. Now that matters had been settled, now that she had nothing else to fear, the only feeling within her heart was one of sheer joy.

"I should very much like to have a small, quiet affair," she murmured, her hands tangling in the back of his hair and making his smile grow steadily. "Not too many guests and the like."

He smiled at her, although his eyes still searched her face. "Does that mean that you—"

"I love you also, Lord Morton," she told him, seeing his sudden delight. "I can think of nothing better than being your wife, for then I shall be able to be in your company whenever and wherever I please." Laughing softly, she stood on tiptoe and pressed her lips to his. This time, Lord Morton's kiss was gentle, his lips soft against hers as he held her close. Emma felt herself melt into him, her happiness now complete.

She would no longer be a part of 'The Spinsters

Guild' for she had found love and loyalty with Lord Morton. In a month's time, she would be wed and be his wife. She could not think of anything more wonderful.

The next book in this series is A Gentleman's Revenge. I hope you enjoy it!

Have you read Book 1 of The Spinsters Guild series? If not, please give A New Beginning a try and find out Lady Smithton's story!

MY DEAR READER

Thank you for reading and supporting my books! I hope this story brought you some escape from the real world into the always captivating Regency world. A good story, especially one with a happy ending, just brightens your day and makes you feel good! If you enjoyed the book, would you leave a review on Amazon? Reviews are always appreciated.

Below is a complete list of all my books! Why not click and see if one of them can keep you entertained for a few hours?

The Duke's Daughters Series
The Duke's Daughters: A Sweet Regency Romance Boxset
A Rogue for a Lady
My Restless Earl
Rescued by an Earl
In the Arms of an Earl
The Reluctant Marquess (Prequel)

A Smithfield Market Regency Romance
The Smithfield Market Romances: A Sweet Regency
Romance Boxset
The Rogue's Flower
Saved by the Scoundrel
Mending the Duke
The Baron's Malady

The Returned Lords of Grosvenor Square
The Waiting Bride
The Long Return
The Duke's Saving Grace
A New Home for the Duke

The Spinsters Guild
A New Beginning
The Disgraced Bride
A Gentleman's Revenge

Love and Christmas Wishes: Three Regency Romance
Novellas

Collections with other Regency Authors
Love at the Christmas Ball
Love, One Regency Spring
Love a Lord in Summer

Please go to the next page for a preview of the first book in The Smithfield Market series, **The Rogue's Flower**!

Happy Reading!

All my love,

A SNEAK PEEK OF THE ROGUE'S FLOWER

"*E*lsbeth?"

Miss Elsbeth Blakely, daughter to some unknown persons and nothing more than an orphan, turned her head to see Miss Skelton enter the room, her thin figure and skeletal appearance matching her name perfectly.

"Yes, Miss Skelton?" Elsbeth asked, getting to her feet as she knew she was expected to, given that this was the lady in charge of the House for Girls. "What can I do for you?"

Miss Skelton, her black hair tied back into a tight bun, gave a small disparaging sniff. "What are you doing in the schoolroom, Elsbeth? The dinner gong has sounded, has it not?"

Elsbeth did not back down, nor feel ashamed of her tardiness. "I have every intention of coming to the dining hall the moment I have finished my letter," she replied, calmly. "After all, was it not you yourself who told me that I was to leave this place just as soon as I could?" She tilted her head just a little, mousey brown curls tipping across her forehead as she did so. Her hair had always been the bane of her life, for she had such tight curls that it was almost impossible to keep them neat and tidy as she was expected to do.

Miss Skelton sniffed again. "That is no excuse, Elsbeth. I expect better from you."

Elsbeth sighed inwardly, aware that Miss Skelton was almost always disappointed with her. Ever since she could remember, Miss Skelton had been a tall, imposing figure that gave her nothing but disparaging and cutting remarks, designed to bring down her confidence. Elsbeth had, in fact, learned how to stand against Miss Skelton's venomous words, shutting down her emotions and closeting away her heart whenever the lady spoke.

"May I ask what letter it is you are writing?" Miss Skelton asked, her hands now clasped in front of her. Her long, grey dress with its high collar that hid most of her neck hung on her like a shroud, giving her an almost death-like appearance that Elsbeth hated so much.

"I have been responding to advertisements regarding governesses," Elsbeth replied, with a slight lift of her chin. "Mrs. Banks has encouraged me in this and I intend to find a position very soon. I do hope that you will give me the references I require." She lifted one eyebrow, a slight challenge in her voice as she waited for Miss Skelton to reply. Mrs. Banks, the lady who taught the girls everything from elocution to grammar, had encouraged Elsbeth in her hopes of making a life for herself outside of the Smithfield House for Girls. Mrs. Banks told her that she had all the knowledge and ability required to become a governess. In a recent spat with Miss Skelton, Elsbeth had been urged to leave the House for Girls as soon as she was able. Miss Skelton pointed out how frustrated she was that she could not throw Elsbeth out on her ear; the two things had come together to encourage Elsbeth to indeed depart. What she required of Miss Skelton was a reference to whichever one of her potential employers wrote back to her with further enquiry.

"I suppose I must," Miss Skelton replied, her voice thin. "If it means that I can get you out of this place, then I will do all I can to help you."

Elsbeth found herself smiling, feeling as though she had won victory. "Thank you, Miss Skelton. It is much appreciated, I am sure." Turning her back on the lady, she sat down again and continued to compose her letter, hearing Miss Skelton's mutter of frustration before she left the room.

Breathing a small sigh of relief, Elsbeth let her pen drift over the page, writing the same words she had written on three other occasions. Her desire to become a governess was growing with every day that she had to spend here. Even though it was the only home she had ever known, it was slowly beginning to suffocate her.

The Smithfield House for Girls was right next to the bustling Smithfield Market, but was in direct contrast to the happiness and warmth that came from there. Elsbeth often spent time looking out of her window to the market place, finding her heart filled with both happiness and pain, wishing that she could have the same joys that was in the faces of so many of those who came to the market.

They laughed and smiled more than anyone ever did in the House for Girls, mostly due to the fact that Miss Skelton was neither happy nor joyful.

Lost in thought for a moment, Elsbeth looked up from her page and let her gaze drift towards the window. Whilst her life had not been altogether bad thus far, the question about where she had come from and why she was here had always dogged her mind. Miss Skelton had never said a word, other than to state that her living allowances had been paid for – and continued to be paid for – year after year. That was why she could never throw Elsbeth out onto the street, since money was sent specifically for Elsbeth's upkeep. Elsbeth could still remember the day she had asked Miss Skelton who sent the money, only for the door to be shut in her face. That had been the day she had begun to dislike Miss Skelton intensely. Elsbeth was frustrated that the woman would not give her any information despite seeing the it upset her to have no knowledge of her birth.

Elsbeth had quietly resigned herself to the fact that she would never know, not unless her father or mother came looking for her. It was an agony that would never fully disappear from her heart, the pain of not understanding why she had been sent here as a baby. Why had her parents had turned her over to Miss Skelton instead of keeping her to raise themselves? She did not understand why Miss Skelton would not speak to her about the matter, did not understand why she would not even explain why she would not do so. That, however, was a burden Elsbeth knew she simply had to bear. Miss Skelton was not about to change her mind, in the same way that she was not about to become a warm and kind-hearted lady who cared about the charges in the House she ran.

That being said, Elsbeth knew that most of the girls here were from noblemen or gentlemen who had chosen to have a tryst outside of wedlock or outside their marriages. It was more than obvious that this was the case, for the girls were trained in all manner of gentle arts, instead of simply being fed and given a place to sleep as they would have done in the poorhouse. There were standards here, standards that both she and the others were expected to meet. Most of them might never know their fathers nor their mothers, but at least their chance at a decent life was much greater than if they'd been left at the poorhouse. There were varying choices for them in their futures – although most would become governesses or teachers in places such as these. Some would become seamstresses, others perhaps marry. Elsbeth winced as she recalled that the annual ball was due to take place in two days' time – a chance for the girls who were out to take part in a small gathering where gentlemen in the lower classes could attend in case they were in need of a wife.... or, perhaps, a mistress. She was revolted at the thought, her eyes closing tightly as she fought against the urge to run away from it all. Being now of age, she had no other choice but to attend, even though she was already responding to advertisements for governesses. Whilst Miss Skelton wanted to be rid of her, Elsbeth knew that it would be in any way she could, which included the ball and a potential husband.

Not that the gentlemen who attended were in any

way nobility. They were mostly baronets, knights, and the like, who were looking for a wife who could fulfill all their requirements whilst still being of decent standing. In addition, Elsbeth knew that many of the girls had a large dowry set aside for them, although none knew from where it had come. That was what brought such gentlemen to the ball, for even though there might be some murmuring over marriages to girls from the Smith-field House for Girls, a gentleman could overlook it should there be a large enough dowry.

Elsbeth had not thought to ask about herself, and was, therefore, quite unaware of any dowry she might have. Perhaps there would be a way for her to hide from most of the gentlemen on the evening of the ball, regardless of whether she had a dowry or not. She did not wish to marry. She wanted to experience life outside of this place, a life where she could earn her own living and make her own way if she chose. Marriage was just another four walls around her, keeping her in line.

Sighing heavily, Elsbeth finished writing her letter, sanded it carefully and then folded it up, ready to be posted.

"Please," she whispered, holding the letter carefully in her hand. "Please, let this be the way out of here. Let me find a new life, far away from Smithfield, London and Miss Skelton. Please." Closing her eyes tightly, she sent her prayer heavenwards before rising from her chair and making her way to the dining room. All she could do now was wait.

CHAPTER ONE

The following afternoon found Elsbeth finishing her embroidery piece, feeling rather pleased with herself. Embroidery had not come naturally to her and yet here she was, finishing off her final piece.

"Wonderful, Elsbeth!" Mrs. Banks exclaimed, coming to sit by her. "You should be very pleased with your work."

"Thank you, Mrs. Banks," Elsbeth replied, with a chuckle. "Although I will say that I do not understand how anyone can find any kind of enjoyment from such a thing."

Mrs. Banks smiled back, her plump face warm and friendly. "Then I should tell you that I do not particularly enjoy it myself, but it is a useful skill to have when one is seeking a husband."

Elsbeth suppressed a shudder. "Thank goodness I am not doing so."

Mrs. Banks nodded slowly. "The ball is tomorrow night. Did Miss Skelton speak to you about it?"

A niggle of worry tugged at Elsbeth's mind. "No, she did not. Why?"

For a moment, Mrs. Banks looked away, her lips thinning and Elsbeth felt herself grow tense.

"You have a large dowry, Elsbeth. I am surprised Miss Skelton has not spoken to you about this before now."

Elsbeth shook her head, firmly. "I do not care. I will not marry."

"I know, I know," Mrs. Banks said softly, putting one gentle hand on Elsbeth's. "But Miss Skelton will be sharing that news with whichever gentlemen show an interest in you at the ball. You must be prepared for that."

Elsbeth felt ice grip her heart, making her skin prickle. "I do not want to marry," she whispered, her embroidery now sitting uselessly on her lap, completely forgotten. "I know Miss Skelton wishes to get rid of me, but I cannot bring myself to preen in front of eligible gentlemen in the hope of matrimony! I want a life for myself."

Mrs. Banks gave her a small reassuring smile, one hand reaching out to rest on her shoulder. "And I am sure you will receive a return to your letters very soon," she replied, calmly, "but you must be aware of what Miss Skelton intends to do. Your dowry is very large, Elsbeth. You have clearly come from a wealthy family."

Putting her head in her hands, Elsbeth battled frustration. So much money, just out of reach. With it, she could do whatever she pleased, set up a life for herself wherever she wanted.

"Although...."

Her head jerked up as she saw Mrs. Banks look from one place to the next, her eyes a little concerned.

"Although?" Elsbeth repeated, encouraging the lady. "Although what, Mrs. Banks?"

Mrs. Banks paused for a moment before shaking her head. "Never mind. It is not something I should say."

Knowing that Mrs. Banks was the closest thing she had to a friend, Elsbeth reached across and took her hand. "Please, Mrs. Banks, tell me whatever it was you were going to say. I feel so lost already. Anything you can tell me will help." Her blue eyes searched Mrs. Banks' face, desperate to know what the lady was holding back.

"I should not be telling you this, Elsbeth," Mrs. Banks replied quietly, "but I have seen how miserable you are here and how Miss Skelton treats you. I am sorry for that. You are a free spirit and she, being as tight-laced as she is, does not understand that. She has never wanted to nurture you, she has simply wanted to contain you, and I cannot hold with that."

A lump in her throat, Elsbeth squeezed Mrs. Banks' hand. "I know," she replied, quietly. "I have valued your teaching and your friendship over the years."

Mrs. Banks drew in a long breath, her shoulders settling as she came to a decision. "As have I," she said, with a great deal more firmness. "Then I shall tell you the truth about your dowry. If you do not marry before you are twenty-one years of age, then the dowry, in all its entirety, goes to you."

Elsbeth gaped at her, her world slowly beginning to spin around her.

"Just think of it, Elsbeth," Mrs. Banks continued

softly, her voice warm. "You need only be a governess for three or four years before you will be truly free. If you are careful, I believe you will have enough to live on for the rest of your days."

Elsbeth could not breathe, her chest constricting. She could hardly believe it, could hardly take it all in, and yet she knew that what Mrs. Banks was saying was the truth. She would not lie to her.

"Why has Miss Skelton never spoken to me about this?" she asked hoarsely, as Mrs. Banks squeezed her hand. "I could have stayed here until...."

"You have answered your own question," Mrs. Banks replied, sadly. "Miss Skelton wants you gone from her establishment and she thought that, in telling you the truth, you would be filled with the urge to remain. There will be funds aplenty until you reach the age of twenty-one, for I am certain that Miss Skelton told me that whoever it is that pays for your board here would do so until either you are wed, or you are twenty-one."

Elsbeth shook her head, fervently. "That cannot be the case. Miss Skelton told me that I must find a place soon as the money that pays for me will soon cease."

"Another lie, I'm afraid," Mrs. Banks said softly, as Elsbeth felt her heart break all over again. "For whatever reason, Miss Skelton is desperate to have you gone from this place. She forbade me to speak of it to you but I knew I could not keep the truth from you. It is too great a truth to have hidden away. It would have been wrong of me to keep it to myself."

Elsbeth drew in breath after breath, her mind whirling as she tried her best to think calmly and clearly about all that had been revealed to her. Miss Skelton had always disliked her but to hide such an enormous truth from her cut Elsbeth to the bone.

"You will have your freedom one day soon," Mrs. Banks promised, putting her arm around her as Elsbeth leaned into her shoulder, just as she might have done with her mother. "Just a few more years."

Trying not to cry, Elsbeth buried her face into Mrs. Banks shoulder. "I do not think I can endure any more time here."

"Then be a governess," Mrs. Banks replied, with a small shrug. "Do whatever you wish, whatever you can until you reach twenty-one. And do not marry a gentleman, whatever you do. I know Miss Skelton is hopeful, but I would encourage you to find a way not to attend the ball tomorrow evening or, at the very least, make yourself as inconspicuous as possible."

Caught by a sudden thought, Elsbeth lifted her head. "You will not get yourself into trouble with Miss Skelton over this? I would hate for you to lose your position."

Mrs. Banks smiled softly, patting Elsbeth's cheek. "You are so caring, my dear. And no, so long as you do not reveal it to her then I think all will be well. Besides which, I do not think that Miss Skelton would dare fire me from this position – for who would she find to replace me? Her reputation as a hard woman, with little care or consideration for anyone but herself is well known." She tipped her head, her eyes alive with mirth. "Do you truly think that she would be able to find another worker with any kind of ease?"

Elsbeth had to laugh, despite her confusion and astonishment. "No, I do not think she would."

"Then you need not worry," Mrs. Banks replied, with a broad smile. "Now, off with you. Go and see if there are any letters that need to be posted so that you might take a turn about the London streets. It might help you think a little more clearly."

"I am rather overwhelmed," Elsbeth admitted, shaking her head. "Thank you for telling me so much, Mrs. Banks. I am indebted to you."

Mrs. Banks smiled again, her eyes suddenly filling with tears. "I shall miss you, when it comes time for you to leave, Elsbeth," she said quietly. "You will promise to write to me, whatever happens?"

Bending down to kiss Mrs. Banks' cheeks, Elsbeth pressed her hands for a moment. "Of course I will, Mrs. Banks. You have made my life so much better here and I will always be grateful for your love and your care for me. Thank you."

CHAPTER TWO

*W*hilst there were no letters to be sent, there was, according to the housekeeper who did the bidding of Miss Skelton, a need for Elsbeth to adorn the front of the House for Girls with flowers. Apparently, it was a reminder to all the gentlemen who had been invited that the ball was to happen tomorrow evening. Elsbeth did not quite understand given that so many of them had already sent their replies to confirm that, yes, they were to attend tomorrow evening's festivities.

Regardless, Elsbeth did as the housekeeper directed without making even a murmur of protest, thinking that to be outside instead of kept within the House would possibly give her the time she needed to think about all that Mrs. Banks had said. She was in no doubt that Miss Skelton had not said as much to her as regards her dowry and the wonderful age of twenty-one when she would attain her freedom, simply because she did not want

Elsbeth to remain in the House for Girls. There had always been something about Elsbeth that Miss Skelton disliked, and now she was making it even more apparent that she did not care for her in the slightest. Whilst Elsbeth knew that she was, as Mrs. Banks had said, a free spirit flying in the face of Miss Skelton's harsh and firmly aligned ways, there had never been any other explanation as to why the lady had taken such a dislike to her. From her earliest memories, Elsbeth could recall Miss Skelton being dismissive and disinterested in her whilst being a *little* more jovial to the other girls. That had only bred anger and resentment in Elsbeth, who had grown more than a little frustrated with the lady's continued dislike of her; so, in her own way, she had done all she could to battle against the lady's hostility, to the point that she knew exactly what to say and do to bring her the most frustration.

Perhaps it was a little childish, Elsbeth reflected, as she picked up the basket which held the brightly colored flowers and the string with which she could tie bunches to the railings that surrounded the House for Girls. Then again, she had been a child for a very long time and only in the last few years had begun the journey towards adulthood. Miss Skelton had never changed, and Elsbeth had felt herself shrinking away from her more and more. She often sought the friendship and understanding of Mrs. Banks, a mother figure to all the orphan girls, and did not think she would have survived life here without her.

But now she had to consider what path to take. She

could remain here until she was twenty-one, in order to come into her fortune, but that would mean over three years of Miss Skelton's dark looks and embittered words. To continue her quest to become a governess seemed the most likely path to take, for then she could simply give up that life when the time came. What would she do then? Where would she go? It was all so unexpected and yet Elsbeth was filled with a delicious excitement. To finally be free, to finally be able to build her own life....it was so near and yet so very far away.

Walking outside, Elsbeth paused for a moment as she took in the bustling market, the laughter and conversations washing over her like a wave of warmth. It was something she longed for but could never have within the House for Girls. Miss Skelton did not even like them to be near to the market, as though afraid they would smile too much for her liking.

Sighing, Elsbeth turned her back to the busy Smithfield Market and focused on her task, hoping she might be able to linger for a little while after she'd finished her task.

"Are you selling these?"

Jerked from her thoughts, Elsbeth turned to see a young man standing a short distance away from her, his eyes bright and a lazy smile on his face. Schooling her features into one of nothing more than general amiableness, she shook her head.

"No, I'm afraid not, sir. I am to place these around the railings." She did not say why, not wanting to encourage the young man to come to the Smithfield

House for the ball, not when he clearly knew this was where she was from.

"I see." He moved closer to her, his smile still lingering – and Elsbeth felt herself shrink back within herself. He was clearly something of a rake, for with his fine cut of clothes and his highly polished boots, there was no doubt that he was a gentleman – and gentlemen, from what she knew, often thought they could get whatever they wished.

He was still watching her intently, his dark brown eyes warm as they lingered on her. His dark hair was swept back, revealing his strong jaw. With his strong back and broad shoulders, Elsbeth was sure that he sent many young ladies hearts beating wildly with hopes of passion, but she had never felt more intimidated.

"Do excuse me," she murmured, making to turn away from him but only for him to catch her elbow.

"Do let me buy one from you," he said, his breath brushing across her cheek. "To remember you by, my fair flower."

Elsbeth felt a curl of fear in her stomach but chose to stand tall, her chin lifted. "No, I thank you, but I cannot sell one to you. I have a job to do. Do excuse me."

She wrenched her elbow from his hand and turned away again, telling herself to remain strong in the face of his oozing self-importance. She did not like him at all, despite his handsome features, for it was clear that he expected a simple compliment to overwhelm her to the point that she would do just as he wished.

"Well, if you will not sell one to me then perhaps you might converse with me for a time," the gentleman continued, his smile a little faded from his expression. "I am greatly inclined to know who you are."

Like what you are reading? Check out the full story in the Kindle Store. If you love a series, here is the link to The Smithfield Market Regency Romance series.

JOIN MY MAILING LIST

Sign up for my newsletter to stay up to date on new releases, contests, giveaways, freebies, and deals!

Free book with signup!

Monthly Facebook Giveaways! Books and Amazon gift cards!
Join me on Facebook: https://www.
facebook.com/rosepearsonauthor

Website: www.RosePearsonAuthor.com
Follow me on Goodreads: Author Page
You can also follow me on Bookbub!
Click on the picture below – see the Follow button?

Made in the USA
Middletown, DE
05 January 2021